I0818277

DON'T FLINCH

(A Taylor Sage FBI Suspense Thriller—Book 4)

Molly Black

Molly Black

Bestselling author Molly Black is author of the MAYA GRAY FBI suspense thriller series, comprising nine books (and counting); of the RYLIE WOLF FBI suspense thriller series, comprising six books (and counting); of the TAYLOR SAGE FBI suspense thriller series, comprising six books (and counting); and of the KATIE WINTER FBI suspense thriller series, comprising nine books (and counting).

An avid reader and lifelong fan of the mystery and thriller genres, Molly loves to hear from you, so please feel free to visit www.mollyblackauthor.com to learn more and stay in touch.

ISBN: 978-1-0943-9523-4

BOOKS BY MOLLY BLACK

MAYA GRAY MYSTERY SERIES
GIRL ONE: MURDER (Book #1)
GIRL TWO: TAKEN (Book #2)
GIRL THREE: TRAPPED (Book #3)
GIRL FOUR: LURED (Book #4)
GIRL FIVE: BOUND (Book #5)
GIRL SIX: FORSAKEN (Book #6)
GIRL SEVEN: CRAVED (Book #7)
GIRL EIGHT: HUNTED (Book #8)
GIRL NINE: GONE (Book #9)

RYLIE WOLF FBI SUSPENSE THRILLER
FOUND YOU (Book #1)
CAUGHT YOU (Book #2)
SEE YOU (Book #3)
WANT YOU (Book #4)
TAKE YOU (Book #5)
DARE YOU (Book #6)

TAYLOR SAGE FBI SUSPENSE THRILLER
DON'T LOOK (Book #1)
DON'T BREATHE (Book #2)
DON'T RUN (Book #3)
DON'T FLINCH (Book #4)
DON'T REMEMBER (Book #5)
DON'T TELL (Book #6)

KATIE WINTER FBI SUSPENSE THRILLER
SAVE ME (Book #1)
REACH ME (Book #2)
HIDE ME (Book #3)
BELIEVE ME (Book #4)
HELP ME (Book #5)
FORGET ME (Book #6)
HOLD ME (Book #7)
PROTECT ME (Book #8)
REMEMBER ME (Book #9)

PROLOGUE

Amy sank her feet in the cool sand and moved across the beach, listening to the waves as they lapped against the shore. Being at her family's beach house on the island was never anything short of peaceful. Stars splashed across the night sky, and she breathed in the clean smell of salt and sea.

It was nice to be alone, but in truth, Amy had stepped out with a hope in mind: to see if the boys hanging out at the other house would be out, to see if Dave would notice her and invite her to hang with them. Earlier, she'd seen the four shirtless guys playing beach volleyball, and she'd wanted more than anything to join in, but her parents had forbidden it. Spending time with Dave had grown increasingly difficult since her mom noticed they'd been seeing each other.

Who am I kidding? she thought to herself. *He's probably not even that into me...*

Amy's eighteenth birthday had just passed, and she'd still never had a real boyfriend, as much as she wanted one. She raked her hands through her long brown hair and wondered if maybe she just wasn't pretty enough to be Dave's girlfriend. Maybe he was just playing her.

Taking a breath, she looked up at the constellations. To Amy, the stars looked like a patchwork of glitter. Their twinkling red, green, and blue lights seemed to be scattered all over the cosmos, and it made Amy feel like she was looking through a telescope, looking at the depths of space.

Suddenly, a sound, like a whoosh, appeared behind her. She looked over her shoulder.

The beach stretched behind her, illuminated only by the moon and stars. Amy swore she saw a shadow in the distance, but she couldn't tell. *Oh well. Probably nothing to worry about.* She'd been living on this island her whole life; it was safe here.

And so Amy kept walking, enjoying the cool sensation of the sand between her toes. The other beach house was only a short walk up.

She glanced over her shoulder again.

The shadow had grown closer.

Its outline was clearer now, a tall, wispy figure. Amy squinted, but she couldn't make out anything else. *It's probably just a trick of the light,* she told herself.

She kept walking. The shadow was still behind her, now on the sand. Amy couldn't see a face, but she swore the figure looked like a man.

Probably a neighbor, she told herself.

Still, she felt her heart beat faster, her palms get sweaty. In most places, walking alone at night was unsafe, but not here.

Right?

She kept walking anyway, taking deep, even breaths. She could make out the other beach house now, the one with the boys.

Amy thought about turning back, but she was determined to say hello to the boys. She just had to get to the other beach house. There would be help there.

Amy looked over her shoulder again—the shadow was closer. It was definitely a man.

Amy picked up her pace, focusing on the other beach house. Then, she heard it: the sound of the boys' laughter. A sense of safety hit her. She just needed to get to them.

She looked over her shoulder, and the shadow was gone.

Whew.

But when she looked in front of her again, a man stood before her with crazed eyes, holding a rag.

Amy stumbled back, ready to scream. But the man grabbed her, covering her mouth. Amy's eyes widened as she struggled, but he had a firm grip.

"Don't scream," he hissed.

Amy couldn't see his face, but something about his eyes gave her the impression that he wasn't sane. She struggled harder.

"Shh," he hissed again. "I just want to help you."

He forced the rag over her face, against her mouth and nose. Amy struggled, but his grip was firm, and the rag was wet. She felt lightheaded.

"Say goodnight, Patricia," was the last thing she heard before the world went black.

CHAPTER ONE

Two things remained in front of Special Agent Taylor Sage's home in Pelican Beach, Virginia: her husband's car, and a FOR SALE sign.

Taylor hugged herself as she waited for Ben to collect the last of his things. Her husband—soon to be ex—came outside with a box and loaded it into the trunk of his hatchback. Taylor avoided looking at him as she stood next to her car on the sidewalk, the late-afternoon sun hot on the back of her neck. It was late-September now, and while the nights were getting colder, the days still held warmth. Taylor dreaded when winter would blow in and chill her to the bone.

Today was the official first day of the house being on the market, and Taylor had come to ensure Ben emptied all of his junk from their home. But to say it had been pleasant would be a lie. Taylor hated the anxiety she felt just being near him.

When Ben slammed the trunk shut, Taylor hesitantly approached him. Ben raked his fingers through his brown hair as he faced her, but avoided her eyes. She ignored the sentimental feeling that tore through her.

"Are you sure that's everything?" Taylor asked coldly. "The realtor is showing the place tomorrow, and they need it clean."

"Yeah," Ben mumbled. "I'm sure."

"Good." Taylor held her arms over her chest. "I'll talk to the realtor about setting up the listing. We were showing off the market, but we'll get it online soon."

"Okay." Ben nodded hesitantly. A few moments passed before Ben cleared his throat. "So, uh... I guess this is it, then."

"I guess so." Taylor tried not to read too much into Ben's tone, but she couldn't help but feel broken as she responded.

Despite everything, Taylor and Ben were being civil throughout their divorce. Nothing had been finalized, but Taylor did not resist signing the papers. She was as done with him as he was with her, and now all that remained was the empty shell of what was once a beautiful marriage. Or maybe it never was beautiful; maybe Taylor had just been blinded.

Ben had always wanted children, and now that it was clear Taylor couldn't give that to him, he was done with her. He had been quick to leave, to throw her away. But Taylor knew she hadn't been perfect in the marriage either. She'd been distant, work-obsessed. When she found out she was infertile, she'd failed to tell him the truth for a couple of weeks, which had put even more strain on their already fragile marriage.

"Thanks for taking this so well," Ben said.

Taylor's eyes flashed against his. Inside, she felt bitter. She couldn't resist the question: "Who is she?"

Ben's eyebrows shot up. "Who?"

Taylor wanted to roll her eyes. Really? He had the audacity to lie? "The woman you were with before you even asked for a divorce," she said flatly.

"That's not fair," Ben said. "I wasn't with anyone."

Ben was lying, and Taylor knew it. She could see it in the way his eyes shifted around. To Taylor, it was more than clear. She had heard the woman's voice in the background of their call.

"You were with someone," Taylor said through her clenched teeth. "Who was she? I have a right to know."

"She was... it was nothing." He averted his eyes like a guilty child, making Taylor's blood boil.

"It was something," Taylor said boldly. "After everything, I think you owe me some truth."

"Forget it, Taylor. There was no one else."

"I know you're lying," Taylor said. "I have the right to know."

Ben's nostrils flared, his face reddening. "Why are you so persistent?"

It was a fair enough question. Taylor didn't need to know, but she felt like after everything, she had the right to know. She'd always been curious by nature, a mystery-solver by trade, and Ben knew that.

"Just tell me who she was," she said.

Ben glared at her for a moment before he answered. "She's… a friend. She's just my friend. There's nothing more to it. My co-worker, Melissa, stopped by the office to drop off some papers, and we got to talking. That's it." He paused. "I didn't do anything while we were still married."

Taylor turned away, her eyes stinging. *While we were still married.* Which meant he had done something since they decided they were divorcing. Technically, they were still married at this moment, but

Taylor wouldn't waste energy on semantics. It wasn't worth it. It didn't matter what the law said; she and Ben were both single.

She heard Ben exhale as he approached her. "I'm sorry. I'm so sorry," he said.

Taylor's chest ached. "No, you're not. You don't even know what that word means."

"I am sorry! I'm sorry I put you through this. I'm sorry I was such a miserable husband. I'm sorry for me and for you. I'm sorry I let things get so out of control."

To Taylor's surprise, Ben pulled her into his arms. She pushed him away and glared at him. His arms weren't home to her anymore. They never would be again.

"I tried so hard to make us work," Ben said in a low voice. "It's my fault."

"It doesn't matter anymore," Taylor said. "I just wanted to know who she was."

No more words were said between them. Taylor turned and walked to her car. She got in, started it, and drove away. As she drove, she couldn't shake the feeling of emptiness that welled up inside of her.

With everything that had gone on between them, she still felt sad to see Ben go. She still loved him, but her love was not the same as it was months ago. It was more like loving the memory of him. Like mourning the death of a loved one. Ben as she knew him was gone, but the good memories—she still loved those.

But like a death, Taylor had no choice but to move on from it. The tides had turned. Both she and Ben had made their choices.

As Taylor drove through Pelican Beach, she thought of the short time she'd spent living here. It had its moments of peace, though few and far between. She drove past downtown and gazed at Miriam Belasco's shop. After what had happened last time, with Miriam going into the trance and drawing the symbol, Taylor had no intention of returning, at least not for a while. She couldn't do that to the poor woman. She wouldn't ask that much. Clearly, Taylor was bad for Miriam's health.

But her heart sank as she drove away. She was going back to Baltimore, back where she grew up.

Still, part of her would miss this idyllic little town. She'd miss the waves by the shore. The boardwalk she could walk on for hours. The touristy shops she never really got around to visiting.

But her time here was over now. It was time to move forward.

***

Hours later, when the late-September sun had set, Taylor walked into her motel in Baltimore. Most of her belongings from the house were in her parents' garage, and she'd been living here like a vagabond since she realized she couldn't stay in her house anymore without thinking of Ben. Being with her parents was an option, and some nights she did stay there—but when she needed to think and be alone, this was where she came.

Taylor turned on the lights and walked deeper into the room.

On the table, she had laid out three things.

One: A picture of the symbol Belasco had drawn. A circle with a squiggled line beneath it.

Two: A piece of paper with the words Belasco had said on it: "Someone is reaching out from across the ocean."

Three: A tarot card. The Moon. Taylor suspected a moon was what was above the ocean in the symbol.

All of these clues, Taylor suspected, would point her to Angie. Her sister who had gone missing two decades ago.

But Taylor wasn't ready to tell her parents, not yet, although she was getting close. This symbol—Taylor had seen it before. She just couldn't place where.

Last week, Taylor had driven around the neighborhood that she and Angie grew up in, searching for the symbol anywhere, but she came up empty-handed. She was taking some time off work under the guise of selling her house in Pelican Beach, but the truth was, Taylor needed a break from the FBI to think about this thing with Angie. She'd be back at work in a few days, but she planned on using this time to get some answers.

And the longer she didn't know, the more she panicked.

But Taylor's day wasn't done.

She picked the tarot card back up, running her fingers over the symbols that made up the image. The Moon. A woman sat under a tree, wrapped in a cloak, with a glowing full moon hanging above.

She was that woman. From the tarot card. Or maybe this was her sister. Angie was the one who took care of her, the one who could calm her down when she was so angry, the one who had to hold her hand when they went out because she was afraid of walking into traffic.

As she sat there, looking at the card, Taylor remembered the last night Angie stayed at home, before she went missing.

Angie and Taylor had been sitting in the living room, watching a movie and eating popcorn with salt and butter. But Taylor had been too angry to enjoy it, pissed off about some friend drama at school that Angie had been helping her through. Taylor had never been a social butterfly, and this was one of the reasons why: her friend, Jane, had been apparently saying bad things behind Taylor's back. Angie had been coaching Taylor on how to deal with it, and her advice basically added up to: *distance yourself.*

The movie ended, and Angie said, "I'm going to bed." And she walked toward the stairs, but Taylor jumped to her feet and stopped her. "Angie, wait!" she called.

Angie turned. "What?"

"Stay here with me. We can watch another movie."

Angie shook her head. "No, I'm tired." Her eyes were too. She always seemed to have dark circles under her eyes from doing homework all the time. Angie had drama in her own friend group too, and with a boy she'd been seeing on and off for a year who was constantly breaking her heart. But tonight, Taylor needed her. She didn't want to think about Jane and all the lies she'd been telling.

"Angie, don't leave me alone. Please."

"Alright, fine." Angie walked back down the stairs. "What do you want to watch? A documentary? A rom-com?"

"I don't care." Taylor had just wanted to spend more time with her sister. She couldn't explain why. At the time, Taylor was fourteen and Angie was sixteen. Now, Taylor was thirty-four—almost thirty-five—and Angie would be thirty-six. Her thirty-seventh birthday was in October.

All these years, Taylor had thought Angie was kidnapped by some sick individual who had a huge infatuation with her. And maybe killed her. But what if it wasn't that? What if Angie ran away? What if she just wanted to be free?

It was a possibility Taylor never considered, but what if she really was out there.

Taylor clenched her fists as she thought of the possibilities. What if she was too late to save her? What if Angie didn't *want* to be saved?

All those years ago, all that was left behind was a shred of Angie's clothing. That was enough for Taylor to believe that something sinister had happened. There was no way Angie would have run away and not contacted their family after all this time. It would be too cruel.

No, if Angie was out there, Taylor was sure someone had to have taken her.

And these clues from Belasco, they had to mean something. Taylor picked up the paper with the symbol of the circle and the squiggle on it. It looked like the moon above the ocean. But it was so familiar. No matter how much Taylor tried to remember, she drew a blank. Taylor had been racking her brain on this for what felt like eons.

Maybe it was time to see if her parents recognized it.

CHAPTER TWO

Taylor pulled her car into her parents' modern, yet cottage-style home. Taylor had to admit, it was nice living closer to Baltimore and D.C.—and her work at Quantico. It had been Ben's idea to move to Pelican Beach. But Taylor was home now, and she was looking forward to finding a place to stay permanently in Baltimore. The plan was to look for a condo, maybe a townhouse, something that wasn't too big. In many ways, she looked forward to having her own space without Ben's clutter.

She walked up to the house and opened the door. Instantly, she was met with the warm smell of her childhood home. Her father was a clinical psychologist while her mother was an artist, and their home had always felt colorful and warm. It was a little later than she normally came here, but Taylor was sure her parents were still up and about.

She walked into the kitchen. Her mom stood at the stove, stirring a pot of tomato sauce for spaghetti. Steam rose from the pot. She was in her sixties now and graying, but still had a youthful demeanor.

"Taylor, what are you doing here?" her mom asked. "Did you forget something in the garage?"

"No, Mom," she said. "I came to see you and Dad."

Her mom turned off the stove and walked over to Taylor, pulling her into a hug. "How are you doing, honey? I didn't know you were coming over."

"I'm doing alright," she said. "I've just been running around trying to find a house and trying to get my stuff in order."

"You could have sold the Pelican house online," her mom scolded. "That would have saved you a whole lot of running around."

"I know, but I wanted to make sure everything went smoothly myself. You know how I am." Taylor paused, emotion thick in her voice. "Ben moved the last of his stuff out today."

Sympathy took over her mom's face. "Oh, honey. You saw him?"

"I did. And the divorce will be finalized soon."

"I'm sorry, honey."

Taylor shook her head. "Don't be. I'm not."

"But you loved him."

"I thought I did," Taylor said. "I thought he was the one. I thought we were going to get married and have kids and grow old like the rest of you." She smiled. "I guess I just wasn't thinking forward enough."

"Taylor, you can't expect everything to work out," her mom said, pulling her into a hug.

"I know, Mom. But it's weird without him around."

"It's going to be strange for a while. But new things are starting for you soon."

"I know." Taylor sighed. "I just want to focus on what's next. I need a fresh start. I want to leave everything behind and just start over. That's why I'm moving back to Baltimore."

"I'm sorry it had to happen like this, but I'm proud of you," her mom said. "Now you can find someone who will treat you right."

Taylor's cheeks flushed. She hadn't even considered the idea of dating. "I don't think I'll be on the market myself for a while, Mom."

"You never know," her mom said. "You're young, you're beautiful, and you've got a good job at the FBI. And the men will be lining up to date you."

"No, Mom," Taylor said. "I'm not even thinking about men right now."

Quite the opposite. Taylor couldn't even imagine letting another man into her bed, let alone her heart. She knew it was common to sleep around after a breakup to help cleanse the former partner from your mind, but Taylor couldn't even imagine it. For so many years, she'd wanted no one but Ben, and soon she'd have to open her mind to the idea of seeing somebody else. Or maybe she could just stay single forever. That didn't sound like the worst plan.

Her mom squeezed her hand. "I just worry about you, honey. You're so independent. You don't need anyone to take care of you."

"I know, Mom," Taylor said. "But I'm a big girl. I can take care of myself."

"Just be careful, honey."

Taylor took a deep breath and let it out. She hadn't come here to talk about her disastrous marriage or the prospect of dating again. Which would maybe never happen, as far as Taylor was concerned. She didn't want to beat around the bush anymore, so she just came out with it:

"Mom, I need to ask you something about Angie."

Her mother's face changed immediately. "What about Angie?" she said, matching Taylor's serious tone.

Taylor pulled out the tarot card and the piece of paper with the symbol on it.

Her mother sighed, sitting down at the kitchen table. "What is this?"

"Did you ever see this symbol before?" Taylor asked. "Maybe on something Angie left behind?"

Her mom frowned, looking at the symbol. "I don't know, sweetie..."

"What's going on?" Taylor's father, Randall, walked in the room. He was normally warm, but something haunted was in his expression as he looked at the documents Taylor had laid out on the table.

"Oh, hi, Dad," Taylor said.

Her dad gave her a brief hug. With knitted brows, he observed the image, the quote, and the tarot card. "What is all this, Taylor?"

Taylor's nerves were frayed. Every time she thought of Angie, she didn't know what to do. She felt like she was going crazy. And voicing these thoughts and feelings to her parents terrified her. She was worried her dad, especially, would believe she had a screw loose.

Plus, the topic of Angie was always a touchy one with him.

But Taylor knew she had to come clean about where this was all coming from. She'd have to confess she'd been visiting a tarot reader, and that it was her who had given Taylor these clues.

Clues that could be related to Angie's disappearance.

"Dad, do you recognize this symbol?" Taylor asked.

"I don't think so." He crossed his arms over his plaid shirt. Some of his gray stubble was growing in. "Why? What is all this?"

Taylor's stomach knotted up. It was time to come clean. "Mom, Dad... I know this is going to sound odd, but... I've been visiting a, well, a tarot reader. And some strange things have been happening that make me believe Angie might still be out there."

Taylor's dad laughed. "You can't be serious."

Her mom just looked away. Taylor's heart sank. Of course they wouldn't believe her. And this was just going to reopen old wounds. Taylor's parents had accepted Angie's disappearance.

But Taylor hadn't.

"I know it sounds crazy," Taylor said. "But Angie could still be alive."

"No, Taylor," her dad said, turning to her. "You have to let her go."

"I can't." Taylor shook her head. "I can't. She's my sister. You both say you know how I am. I have to know if my sister is out there."

"We just want you to find happiness, Taylor," her mother said. "This won't bring Angie back."

"Why are you—how did you—" Taylor didn't know what to say. "You don't believe me."

"No, Taylor, it happened years ago," her dad said. "Angie isn't coming back. It's been twenty years."

"Taylor, honey," her mom said, "if Angie was alive, she would have contacted us. She would have let us know that she was okay."

"But what if she can't? What if someone has taken her? What if she's being kept somewhere?"

Taylor could feel her mom's and dad's eyes on her, but she couldn't look at them.

"What if she's running from something?" she said. "Or what if she just doesn't want to be found?"

Her mother got up from the table, tears in her eyes. "Taylor, please. Don't say that. You know how this upsets your father."

"I know, Mom, but think about it! Angie and I were close. She would have contacted us. If someone took her, she would have let us know. I know she would have."

Her dad sighed. "I understand you're having a hard time, Taylor, but this isn't the way. You've been seeing some tarot reader? What is that all about?"

Taylor hated this. It was her worst fear coming to life. Of course her parents would think she was crazy. Hell, sometimes Taylor thought she was crazy herself. But she'd seen for herself the way Belasco could predict things—the way those things could come true.

"Will you please just hear me out?" Taylor said. "I know the tarot stuff sounds insane, but you know me. I promise I wouldn't be entertaining it if it wasn't compelling."

Taylor's mom exchanged a look with her dad before she sighed. "Randall, maybe we should hear her out... you know I've always been a bit spiritual."

"Linda, don't entertain this!" Randall exclaimed. He was beginning to grow red in the face, and Taylor worried about his blood pressure. "You can't go believing your daughter's fantasies. It's been twenty years. Don't you think it's time to let go?"

Taylor watched her parents argue back and forth. She couldn't remember the last time she'd seen them argue like this. It made her feel like a child again, not a thirty-four-year-old woman.

"That's why I want to find her," Taylor cut in. "To prove to you that she's not a fantasy."

"We just want you to be happy, sweetie," her mom said, coming over to her and touching her hand. "It's been so long since you've been happy. Do you think I haven't noticed?" Taylor's mother sat down at the table again, leaning in. "Taylor, tell us everything."

At this point, she had opened the floodgates. And so she told them everything. How she'd been to the tarot reader's shop and how the reading had made her question everything. How the tarot reader had even helped nudge her in the direction of clues in cases she was working. How all of it had made her start to believe that maybe there is more out there, things we can't see or understand.

As she spoke, her mom rubbed her arm and her dad stared into space. It was clear he was in a bad mood.

Finally, Taylor stopped talking. "So now I don't know what to do. I know everything sounds crazy, but there has to be some truth to it. I just can't shake the feeling this means something."

"Well, I actually think it's a bit interesting," her mom said. A smile took over her face. "Maybe there is hope for Angie. We never found her body, so—"

Taylor's dad's fist slammed against the table, shocking everyone. The hair on Taylor's neck rose. Her father had rarely, if ever, shown any signs of violence or frustration like this. "Enough, damn it!" her dad shouted. "Taylor, don't give your mother false hope! Do you have any idea how difficult it has been to accept our daughter is dead?"

Taylor was devastated. She didn't know what to say. "But Dad—"

"No buts! This is ridiculous! This is—"

Her dad made a sudden choking sound, his eyes bulging. He grabbed at his chest. Panic flooded Taylor’s mind. What was wrong with him? Was he hurt? Taylor and her mom rushed to his side as he retched in pain.

"What happened?" her mom asked.

"I don't know," her dad said, looking down at his hands. "It's like I can't breathe..." Randall rested his head on the table, grunting in pain.

"Oh my God!" Taylor cried. "What's happening?"

"I think he's having a heart attack!" her mom said. "Help! Someone help! 911! We need an ambulance!"

Before Taylor knew what was happening, her mom was on the phone with 911. She screamed into the phone as her dad cried out in pain on the floor. It all felt like a sick and twisted dream. Taylor loved her father. This couldn’t be happening. Just when Taylor thought she was going to faint, her dad's breathing slowed, and his eyes closed.

Soon, the sound of the ambulance sounded outside, and paramedics rushed in. Taylor's world seemed to move in slow motion as they gathered her father and put him on a cot, taking him outside of the house.

Taylor's world crumbled around her.

CHAPTER THREE

The silence in the hospital hallway was like a deafening noise in Taylor's ear. She had caused all this. She had stressed out her father and now he was here, in the hospital, waiting to hear what was wrong with his heart. This was all her fault.

The chairs in the hall were empty but one... occupied by her mother, who would not meet Taylor's eyes. Taylor knew she was ashamed of the way she had spoken to her father tonight. On a day like today, she wished her mother had been firmer with her, or that Taylor hadn't been so difficult. It hadn't occurred to Taylor until it was too late that their arguing might be causing further damage to her father's heart. In many ways, stress could be the worst poison of all.

She sat still for a moment in one of the empty chairs, and once more tried to suppress the feeling of guilt which now came welling up in her throat. She tried to swallow it down, but it stuck there, like a physical thing in the pit of her stomach. She crossed and uncrossed her legs, trying to get comfortable sitting on the chair; she was so nervous that her muscles trembled.

"Taylor," her mom said.

Taylor's eyes snapped to her. "What?"

"Stop fidgeting. You're going to work yourself into a sweat."

"But—"

Just then, the doctor emerged from the doorway. Taylor and her mother stood at attention, necks strained. The air in the room felt heavy, charged. Their breathing had stopped, along with the whole world. So much rested in that moment—the fate of the Sage family rested on the next words from the doctor's mouth. In his early thirties, with a round face and soft eyes that squinted through tiny, round glasses, Dr. Bloom crossed his arms over his chest. His scrubs were white, crisp, and symbolized hope.

After what seemed like an hour, but was really only thirty seconds, Dr. Bloom finally spoke up.

"He's going to make a full recovery," he said.

Both Taylor and her mom let out a sigh of relief. Thank God. If Taylor had seriously hurt her dad, she never would have been able to forgive herself.

"But his body did sustain some damage," Dr. Bloom continued, "and he's going to need to take it a bit easy."

While her mother and the doctor spoke, Taylor stood still. She felt bad for having yelled at her dad. She thought she heard the doctor asking questions about her dad, but then she couldn't make out anything else.

In this dreamy state, Taylor tried to tell herself that everything had turned out okay. But that didn't soften the blow of finding out that her father wasn't well.

"When can we see him?" her mom asked.

"He's sleeping right now," the doctor said. "You can see him tomorrow, but right now he needs to rest."

The doctor excused himself, and Taylor and her mom went back into the waiting area. Both of them took seats.

"He's going to be okay," her mom said. "We did it."

Taylor looked over to her mom, who smiled at her. Taylor couldn't resist the emotion that struck her. She wanted to cry, but held it in as best as she could.

"I'm so sorry, Mom," she said.

"Honey, why?" her mom asked.

"It's my fault."

"What? No, it's not. I told him he was eating too much salty food..."

Taylor shook her head. "If I hadn't stressed him out, this wouldn't have happened. I never should've brought Angie up."

Taylor's mom's hand quickly grabbed hers, and she squeezed. She looked her in the eyes and said, "Taylor, you're my daughter—I know you. I know you wouldn't have looked into this if it wasn't serious. I don't want you to hurt yourself, but if you believe Angie is out there, then I have faith in your belief."

Taylor wiped her eyes. She really wanted to believe her mom.

"Besides, how many lives have you saved? How many cases have you solved? It's all proof that you can do it." Her mom smiled warmly. "So go do it."

Taylor's mom let go of her hand, and Taylor wiped her eyes again. She nodded. Her mom was right. For as long as Taylor had been in the FBI, she felt like her life had purpose. Real purpose. That was why she'd always been absorbed in it, sometimes at the cost of her personal relationships. Taylor knew that could be selfish, and maybe it was; but she was saving lives, and at the end of the day, that was all that mattered to her.

If she could save Angie's, then it would be the ultimate win.

"I will," she whispered.

***

Back at her motel room, Taylor slumped against the chair at the table with the clues laid out in front of her: the moon and wave symbol, the quote, and The Moon tarot card.

She felt like a true piece of garbage for stressing out her father, and no amount of kindness from her mother could erase that guilt. But still. Taylor had to keep her resolve intact. Maybe Taylor was letting herself get carried away on a wave of emotion—but nevertheless, ever since the clues from Belasco, her senses had never been so sharpened before.

Her thoughts were more developed than ever before. Her energy levels were through the roof, and for the first time in her life, she felt driven by an almost supernatural force to find out whether or not there was something more powerful than herself out there in the universe. Something that could help her bring Angie home.

She knew her dad wouldn't understand now. But if Taylor could find Angie, it would all be worth it. He would forgive her. They would be a family again.

Sitting in the half-light of the motel room, she smiled to herself, imagining what it would be like to have her sister home after two decades. What type of woman she might be? The family dinners they might have. She pictured herself, Angie, and their parents, at their dining room table again on Christmas, in the glow of the Christmas tree.

A cautious voice emerged in Taylor's mind. Her practical self, her old self, who didn't believe in tarot and psychics or any of that stuff. The voice said:

Be careful. You don't know for sure she's out there.

She could be dead.

You will suffocate on this if she is.

Taylor's heart hurt just thinking about that. She'd grown so hopeful and optimistic that it scared her.

Maybe she was delusional.

Maybe her father was right.

But it didn't matter. She was already in this, and she had to stay focused.

She looked at the clues again. So, her parents didn't recognize the symbol. But the quote—it had to mean something.

"Someone is calling for you from beyond the ocean."

Another continent?

Or an island?

Island...

Taylor thought back, a jolt of familiarity hitting her.

It had been so long since Taylor had thought about this place. But just off the coastline, there was an island where her parents used to rent a cottage/beach house for them to visit in the summer. Brock Island. They'd only stay for a week at a time, and they stopped going before Taylor was in high school.

But at the age of twelve or thirteen, she remembered. Taylor and Angie were walking along the beach. The tide had been really far out, and the moonlight reflecting off of the water turned everything a glowing misty silver color. The sight of it had put her sister in awe. Angie had turned and pointed at the water, and said something along the lines of: "It's beautiful. It's calling to me. I want to swim in it."

Taylor, young and curious and a kid, nodded. "Really?"

Angie smiled. "Yes... even when it's cold."

Taylor remembered glancing over her shoulder to the rocks off the shore, where someone had graffitied something in white paint.

A circle... and a squiggled line...

"Angie, look," Taylor had said, "I think it's the moon and the ocean." Her sister's heart-melting, dreamy smile... her smile... in that moment, she'd wanted to do anything for her sister.

And then Taylor had forgotten. She had never gone back there again. Never told anyone else. Never connected it to the moon and ocean symbol or quote.

Taylor snapped out of her reverie; her eyes popped open. She felt nauseous with excitement.

The image of the symbol in her memory was vague. Blurry. Was it even real? The memory felt so distant, yet so vivid, but the fact that Taylor had not thought of it until now scared her. Scared her that she was descending into madness and fabricating memories to validate her own delusion.

She recalled her father's reaction to the symbol; he had looked pale, like he'd seen it before, even though he said he hadn't.

It's real, Taylor thought. *It has to be.*

But there was only one way to find out.

First thing in the morning, Taylor was returning to Brock Island. She would search every inch of that island, and hopefully, she would find out once and for all if she was going insane or not. She had to know for sure. She had to learn everything about that beach, about that cottage, about that—

Childhood, a voice in her head sighed.

And a sister long-lost...

The moon and the ocean...

Angie and Taylor.

And all the hope that came with it.

CHAPTER FOUR

First thing in the morning, Taylor took the ferry across the bay to Brock Island. The faint rays of the sun were just cresting over the horizon. There was no line of demarcation between water and sky. The water rose and fell like great, gentle swells of gauzy blue-gray. Cool ocean breezes flowed through her hair as she sat in the boat. Blue water stretched out around her, going in every direction as far as she could see.

It was beautiful. And as the ferry continued on its slow zigzag course toward the island, it reminded Taylor of the countless times she'd watched the ferry pass by the island from the shore.

The sound of the wheel churning in the water was hypnotic. She kept her eyes on the ocean. She kept seeing flashes of the symbol, her sister's image, the moon and the ocean. She was sure of it.

She didn't know why it was coming back to her now, but she knew that it was. Taylor had a feeling. Everything in her life was bringing her to this moment.

As the boat was docking, she stepped onto the island and looked around. It was a touristy spot, well-populated and idyllic, although Taylor remembered there were a lot of locals who lived here permanently, year-round.

If the rock with the symbol was still there, she was going to find it.

After a long night of little sleep, Taylor was too frazzled to think straight. But she didn't care. She had to find that spot on the beach. The island wasn't huge, and the rock must have been near where the old cottage was. Taylor's legs moved for her. Hot sand pressed beneath her shoes, and she regretted not wearing sandals; she was too used to dressing up for the FBI, in long pants and black shirts and shoes.

She walked for a while around the coastline, and as she got farther from the ferries and shops, she started to feel isolated. Then she turned down an area that was empty, and she felt even more isolated. There was no one else around. No comfort.

All that mattered was finding that symbol.

And then she came to a spot that felt eerily familiar. Deeper into the shore, she could make out the shape of the old cottage her family used to rent. It struck her with nostalgia. Paddle boats and kayaks were in the sand in front of the house. She was getting close.

Taylor walked further up the beach.

The smell of the ocean, the silhouette of the water...

She remembered that night, walking with her sister, looking at the stars.

Taylor felt a jolt. A sense of déjà vu. A sense of longing.

The sandy area around her was generic, but up ahead, on the shoreline, was a series of dark rocks.

That had to be where she'd seen the symbol.

Heart in her throat, Taylor ran up to it, not caring about the hot sand leaking into her shoes and socks. The gritty sensation was uncomfortable, but Taylor pushed on until she reached the rocks.

She looked around, desperately, for the graffiti.

The rocks were smooth, a dark black-gray color. No symbols. Just some teenaged kids' names—and two people named Theresa and Greg. Taylor walked around, looking at every inch of the large rock, and nothing.

Taylor sighed. She'd been so sure about this. So sure that the symbol was here. So sure that this was the right place.

Maybe she'd just forgotten. Maybe she'd just made it up.

In a panic, Taylor felt her own heart lurching in her chest. The symbol was not here. She gasped for air and tried to breathe, but she was having difficulty. There was no way to tell for sure if the symbol was real.

What if her memory wasn't real?

What if her sister wasn't alive?

That last question made Taylor's heart crumple. She closed her eyes and tried to gasp for air, but her breath was still coming in ragged, shallow bursts, and the waves of sadness were crashing against her chest. She tried to breathe.

No, she thought. *No.*

There was no proof.

No proof.

But she had to get out of here. She couldn't stand it. She'd come to this place for answers, and now she had none. She turned around and ran back up the beach, away from the cottage and the beach and the ocean. She ran back toward the shops and the ferries. She didn't care how hot her feet were from the sand; it was worth it to get away.

She ran back toward the path she'd taken to get here, but she didn't want to go back that same way; she couldn't face the cottage again. She jogged in the opposite direction, past the shops and the ferries, past the paddle boats and kayaks. She walked along the coastline to the other side of the island, the wilder side.

She was staring at the water and sand.

Still, no answers.

It all felt so fruitless. She was chasing a ghost, wasn't she? She'd come all this way, and for what? A hunch? She really was going crazy.

Taylor felt darkly depressed as she walked back toward the ferries, taking a detour through town, past the small touristy shops. As she did, she noticed a commotion of people gathered outside of the police station. Taylor remembered walking down this strip with her family, eating ice cream. Angie's favorite had been plain vanilla.

As she drew closer to the crowd, she made out some voices. It was a group of citizens shouting at a man in a police uniform.

"Where is Amy Schuler?" one woman shouted. "Have you found her yet?"

"Are our kids in danger!?" another person screamed.

"Please, calm down," the officer said, holding his hands up. "We are doing everything we can to locate the missing girl."

A missing girl? Taylor thought. This was ringing too many bells for her. She approached the scene and pushed her way through the crowd, taking out her FBI badge—she never left her home without it, even when she was off-duty. She never knew when she might need to prove her identity, and right now, it was coming in handy.

"I'm FBI," she said quickly. "I need to get through."

The crowd parted for her, looking around and whispering.

The police officer stood tall and stared at her. "You're with the bureau? Were you sent here?"

"I'm just visiting," Taylor said. "There's been a kidnapping? In town?" This community was too small for something like that to happen unnoticed.

The policeman shook his head. "No, it's not that. It's just, a girl went missing. She's a teen. Her name is Amy Schuler. She went missing two nights ago."

"Who reported it?" Taylor asked.

"Her parents. They've lived here forever."

A citizen jumped in and said, "They still haven't found her!"

"Ma'am, we are working on it," the officer cut in.

Taylor glanced over her shoulder at the overeager and anxious crowd. She faced the officer, whose badge read Brady. This wasn't her case, but Taylor couldn't resist; she needed to know more about this Amy Schuler.

"You have somewhere private we can talk?" Taylor asked. "I need to ask you some questions."

Brady nodded and led Taylor into the police station. The station was small and old, with wooden desks and staircases, and the walls were lined with old photographs. It felt more like a museum than an actual police station, but Taylor knew a place like this would mostly just bust underage drinkers on the island. Brady led her into a small office and sat behind his desk, which had a framed photo of a young girl on it. Taylor sat opposite him.

"What brings an FBI agent here?" Brady asked.

"I was just... looking for something," Taylor said. "But what's going on with the missing girl? Got any leads?"

"No. We've searched the island and the sea. We've talked to the ferry workers, and they say they saw her the day she went missing. But she didn't come back."

"Do her parents remember what she was wearing?"

Brady shook his head. "The father said she left their house wearing a white shirt, jeans and a pair of sandals. A red sweatshirt, too. It gets cool at night."

"And that was two nights ago?"

Brady nodded. "We've put out a missing persons alert, but no one on the island has seen her."

Taylor began to feel sick with nostalgia, remembering how it had felt in those first forty-eight hours after Angie went missing. You still cling onto hope at first.

"Where was she last seen?" Taylor asked.

"On the beach."

Taylor nodded. "And was there any evidence left behind?"

"Only one thing," the officer said. "A shred of clothing from the sweatshirt she was wearing."

Taylor's heart stopped.

A shred of clothing...

That was exactly what had been left behind when Angie went missing.

"Do you have it?" Taylor asked.

"It's in evidence on the mainland," Brady said. "Look, there are only three cops looking after this island... we don't deal with stuff like this. When I saw you were FBI, I was hoping you'd been sent to help, but I guess this isn't a big enough case for you guys yet. I mean, maybe the girl ran away with a boy. We just don't have the details yet."

"Right," Taylor said. "Right." Her mind was racing a mile a minute. She couldn't jump to conclusions. The evidence could be unrelated. But Taylor's detective instincts were telling her something here.

She needed to see that evidence. But getting to the mainland and interfering could take too much time.

"Do you have a photograph of the piece of clothing left behind?"

"Actually, I do," Brady said. Hope leapt in Taylor's chest. He took out his phone and showed her an image. It was a rectangular shred of clothing.

Taylor had memorized the shred that had been left behind when her sister went missing.

Because it was all of Angie that had remained. Her entire life, boiled down to one shred of clothing.

There had been something strange about it; it looked as though it had almost been torn intentionally off her sweater, in a sort of rectangular shape just like the one she was seeing now.

Taylor was having trouble breathing.

She felt very hot, and she knew she was sweating. Even though she didn't have her jacket on, she was burning up. She felt dizzy, and she could hear her own heartbeat in her ears.

She leaned forward and put her head between her legs.

She felt Brady's hands on her shoulders. "Hey, are you okay?" he asked. "I don't know why you're visiting, but you don't look so good. Come on. Let's get you some water."

Taylor shook her head. She didn't trust herself to speak. Her hand was shaking as she reached into her pocket and turned on her phone.

The officer was talking to her, but she didn't understand it. She could hardly hear anything over the sound of her heartbeat filling her ears.

"What are you thinking?" Brady asked, running a hand along his gruff face. He looked like he'd spent far too much time in the sun. "You look nervous. You're not thinking something crazy, are you? Like, that the girl was taken by a serial killer?"

"No... I'm... I'm thinking that..." The words wouldn't come out.

What she was thinking was that this case was too similar to Angie's.

What she was thinking was that Amy Schuler was taken by the same man.

Taylor knew it was outrageous. She knew she couldn't bring this to the FBI, not without more proof. Girls go missing all the time. And a piece of clothing was probably not enough.

But to Taylor, it was everything.

She needed help on this one—help from a friend.

And she knew just who to call.

CHAPTER FIVE

Special Agent John Wesley turned on the espresso machine in his suburban house and breathed in the warm smell of roasting coffee. Black, just the way he liked it. The early-morning sun poured through the windows, and he glanced out at his yard. There was an above-ground pool, a white picket fence, a trampoline for Maisie and her friends. Wesley didn't have much of a reason to go back there other than to mow the lawn. Everything he did, he did for his daughter.

"Dad, that smells like crap," his daughter, Maisie, said. Wesley turned to see her sitting at the kitchen table, scribbling in her notebook.

"How's the math, kiddo?" Wesley asked, ignoring her remark.

"Stupid," Maisie said.

"It's not stupid; you just have to try a bit harder."

Maisie pouted. "If you're so smart, why don't you do it for me?"

Wesley laughed once. Kids. Damn. They grew up too fast. Wesley remembered when he could hold his baby girl in one hand. Now, at ten years old, she was big enough to sass him. It seemed like it all had happened in the blink of an eye.

Wesley leaned over his daughter's notebook. "Let me see what you've got here." He took a pencil from her fingers and gave the page a quick once-over. "You're not getting it. Show me what you got there."

"I got the first part. The second part is just a big long equation, but I don't know what the answer is at the bottom of the page."

Wesley nodded. "Okay. Let's get that bottom part out of the way. What's the key in the problem?"

"I don't know," Maisie said. "How could I know that?"

"It's okay, sport. Don't get frustrated." Wesley took her pencil and pointed to the part of the equation that she'd been stuck on. "Just look over here. All the numbers added together come to three. So, we can say this is our key. Whatever adds up to three is going to be our key."

"I hate math," Maisie muttered.

Maisie stood. She was wearing a purple dress with yellow flowers. Wesley was proud of her. She was growing up to be a smart, beautiful young lady. Wesley swallowed hard when he remembered that he had to get back to work soon, and that he'd have to let his ex take Maisie.

Maisie hated staying with her mom. Her mom's house was loud and boisterous with music and the TV always blaring, while Wesley's place was as still and quiet as a lake in the dead of night. Wesley enjoyed silence as much as his daughter. But when he was working all the time, he just couldn't always be there to take her to school and pick her up. That left his ex to do most of the parenting, which was the last thing he wanted to admit.

"How about I make some pancakes for you?" Wesley asked.

Maisie nodded, still pouting. But Wesley knew his daughter; she was eager for pancakes, even if she tried to pretend like she wasn't.

Wesley walked to the pantry. Betty Crocker was probably for the best. Maisie had enough excitement for one day. Her little head looked so serious, her brown eyes filled with the weight of the world. She needed a serious breakfast. Pancakes were fun, but they wouldn't do much to fill the growing girl. A box of chocolate cake mix would do the job nicely and had always been Maisie's favorite. If he mixed the cake mix with the pancake mix, he could make her favorite chocolate cake pancakes.

He set everything aside and sat next to Maisie. She smiled brightly at him. He smiled back. But the memory of what he had to tell her today gnawed at his happiness.

He couldn't keep this from Maisie. He'd have to tell her the truth.

"You know," Wesley said, "I have something to tell you."

Maisie sighed. "I have to go stay with Mom again, don't I?"

Wesley almost laughed. She was the daughter of an FBI agent—of course she was perceptive.

"Yeah, kiddo. Sorry. I've gotta get back to work tomorrow. I can't be there to take you to school."

"What if I just stay at a friend's place until you're home from work? Then you can pick me up there?" She blinked at him with big brown eyes.

"Sorry, Mais. You know my hours are all over the place."

Maisie sighed. "I know..."

He ruffled her curly brown hair. "But I'll see you soon. Promise."

Suddenly, Wesley's phone rang. He stepped into his living room, expecting it to be his boss, Winchester.

But it was Taylor Sage.

Wesley lifted an eyebrow. He thought Sage was off work. So why the personal phone call? Wesley had only worked one case with Taylor Sage as his partner, but he felt like they'd each earned a mutual respect for one another. He admired her tenacity and how she always trusted her gut.

Sitting against the arm of his couch, he answered the call. "Sage, what's going on?"

"Hey, Wes," she said. "You busy?"

"Not at this exact moment. Shoot."

Taylor hesitated. "I... I need your help."

Wesley rose and went back to the kitchen to make some more coffee. There was no way he could think with his ten-year-old daughter around. "What's going on?"

"I'll tell you when you're here."

"No," Wesley said. "Tell me now. What's going on? You in trouble?"

"No. Nothing like that. I've just... got a case."

"I didn't get a call about a case."

"It's a little off the books."

Off the books? The hell was Sage talking about? He knew she could be a bit eccentric sometimes, behind her stony exterior, but this was unorthodox.

Either way, she had his attention. This was something he needed to see for himself. He knew that Sage wouldn't call him out of work hours like this if it wasn't a big deal, and he could tell by the tone of her voice that it was serious.

"Just tell me where to meet, and I'll be there," Wesley said.

***

When Wesley got off the ferry at Brock Island, Taylor Sage was waiting on the shore for him. The ocean licked the shore. A gurgling, burbling, clicking sound that was gentle enough to relax and calming enough to settle his nerves. Wesley's mouth felt dry. Maybe he needed some more coffee.

He'd never mistake Taylor's look—a slender, five-foot-four woman with hair as black as the night and eyes a steely gray-blue. She had bangs across her forehead and a hardened expression. Although she was dressed in suit pants with a black shirt, Taylor's ensemble was less formal than usual. A pair of wide-leg pants and shoes.

Truthfully, Taylor was a gorgeous woman, but she seemed not to be aware of that at all. Wesley liked that about her. She was practical, focused on her work, and a damn good agent. At the same time, sometimes Wesley could see she was a bit lost in her head. There was a lot he didn't know about her, and he wondered if today would reveal more. That alone would be enough to get him to follow her into whatever mess they were about to get into.

"Sage," Wesley said as he walked up. Taylor gave him a tight-lipped smile.

"Thanks for coming, Wes."

"What's going on? It's hot as Hades out here."

"Let's go somewhere more private."

Taylor started down the shore, and Wesley followed. The sand felt hot beneath his feet. It didn't take long for them to pass by the town, which was full of tiny shops. The sea lapped the shore, and the waves spread white foam to the frothy water's edge. The rocky spires of the islands rose beyond. They appeared to be made of pure glass, and the sun burned their tips into the air. They glowed and reflected the light, and seemed to shine from within, as if a thousand mirrors lay behind them.

Nice place and all, but Wesley was more concerned about why Taylor had brought him here off the books.

"What's going on, Sage?" Wesley asked.

"Well... a girl went missing here," Taylor said.

"You said this was off the books."

Taylor nodded. "It is. This isn't an FBI case. At least not yet."

"So why the hell am I here?"

Taylor stopped. They faced each other on a secluded part of the beach. The wind brushed the sand across the beach into a constant, steady stream. Taylor squinted into the sun as she looked up at him.

"Wesley, this is going to sound insane, but I think the case here, with the missing girl… it could be big. And it's a bit personal for me."

Wesley lifted an eyebrow. What was she talking about? "Personal how?"

Taylor drew a breath. She was hiding something—Wesley could tell. He waited for her to come clean.

"Let's just say I've dealt with missing girls before," Taylor eventually said.

Vague. Frustrating. But Wesley expected no less from Taylor Sage. Taylor wasn't like most women—she was a bit of a mystery. Mysterious on purpose.

Wesley didn't like secrets, though. Not the secrets friends kept from each other. Not the kind of secrets people in the government kept from others. And definitely not the secrets bad people kept from people who wanted to know the truth.

"Look, you can't tell me and expect me to leave this where it is, Sage," Wesley said.

"I'm not asking you to leave it alone," Taylor said. "I'm asking you to investigate it with me. Help me get to the truth."

For a second that seemed to stretch on for an eternity, Wesley was silent. He knew Taylor was mysterious for a reason. She didn't trust easily. But if he was going to be her partner, he had to know when she was lying. He had to know all the time.

All that aside, this was worth looking into if she'd called him here. He could deal with getting it on the books later. First, he needed the details.

"What's the story on the girl who disappeared?"

Taylor's posture relaxed, but she wasn't off the hook yet. "Amy Schuler, eighteen. She vanished from the beach two nights ago. The only trace left of her was a shred of clothing. An officer told me there was no DNA on it that didn't belong to her."

"And how do they feel about the FBI sniffing around where we weren't invited?"

"Fine so far."

"I'm surprised. So what's the story on this beach? It seems like a pretty nice place," Wesley said.

Once again, Taylor looked like she was holding back. She didn't like to talk about her past.

"Let's just say I spent some time here."

"Sage, what aren't you telling me?"

"Nothing, Wesley."

Wesley put his hands on his hips and sighed, glancing out at the ocean. At least the scenery was nice. And the story did compel him, that was for sure; a missing teenage girl... if anything ever happened to Maisie, he'd destroy Hell and Earth to get her back. And he understood why Taylor would want to get involved, considering small-time cops often didn't have the training to solve a case like this. They'd have to report what they were up to eventually, but for now, Wesley was willing to help Taylor poke around.

But he also wanted to know the truth about why this was so "personal" to her. That was a story he intended to crack.

"All right, I'm in," Wesley said.

Taylor gave him a smile, and something passed between them. Her icy exterior seemed to break for a moment. She was an odd woman, to be sure, but in a good way. Wesley liked working with her so far. He wouldn't put his neck out for many people outside of his blood, but Taylor had been rock-solid on their last case; the least he could do was give her a chance and have her back.

"So," he said, "where should we start?"

CHAPTER SIX

Taylor led Wesley through the streets of downtown Brock Island. They turned a corner and passed by the police station. The citizens who'd gathered earlier had gone, and now the place was back to looking like nothing but a tourist trap. Taylor was still reeling from her nerves over not telling Wesley about Angie—with the way he'd looked at her, gray eyes blazing, she'd almost cracked and told the truth. But she wasn't an open book; Wesley knew that. She was thankful he was willing to work with her for now. But she reminded herself that Wesley was an agent too; surely, his curiosity would win, and he'd find out the truth eventually.

One day, maybe soon, Taylor would tell him about Angie. For now, she just wanted to focus on the case.

Taylor was hoping to talk to Officer Brady again, but when they entered the police station, a different man with an air of authority was pacing out. They all nearly bumped into each other. He wore a sheriff's badge, so Taylor could only assume this was Brock Island's head honcho. His badge read Garth.

"Can I help you folks?" He was gruff-looking with a bald head, a prominent nose, and a deep frown.

"I'm Special Agent Taylor Sage—I work for the FBI," Taylor said. "I'd like to know about the missing person's case."

The sheriff's frown deepened. "Oh, yeah, I heard you feds were sniffing around here. I'm afraid I can't give you that information, Special Agent Sage, and Officer Brady shouldn't have been talking to you either."

Taylor's eyes narrowed. Something was off. "Why is that?" she asked.

The sheriff raised a thick eyebrow. "Our missing persons' cases are closed to the public. Sorry."

"I'm not public. I'm an FBI agent. I just need some information."

The sheriff's frown turned into a scowl. "What are you saying, exactly?"

Taylor stared at him for a long moment, then finally said, "I'm saying you have a missing girl on your hands here and if we act fast, maybe we can find her alive."

Garth's eyes hardened against Taylor's. His silence frustrated her. Thankfully, Wesley stepped in.

"Look, bud, we're with the FBI," he said, flashing his own badge. Wesley was a giant of a man, as tall as he was muscular, and he generally intimidated almost everyone he came in contact with. Taylor knew he was a bit of a softie inside, but Sherriff Garth didn't know that. "We're just here to help out, and considering the state of this place..." Wesley glanced around the room. It was empty, not even a secretary behind the desk. "You look like you could use the extra help."

"I don't want any FBI agents bumbling around here," the sheriff spat. "This is my case. Leave it be."

Taylor bristled. She was confused by the sheriff's reaction. What was he hiding? There was clearly something fishy going on here.

"What's your name, Sheriff?" Taylor asked with venom.

The sheriff scowled at her. "Garth. Sheriff Joe Garth. I'm the man in charge here."

"Then I suggest you not put a roadblock in front of me. If you have a problem with the FBI, take it up with the people upstairs, or just let us help out."

Sheriff Garth huffed. "Fine. This ain't worth my time. I'm at a loss for what to do, anyway." He let out a sigh. "Officer Brady is out looking for the Schuler girl, and I've got a town full of folks panicking. I have zero leads and no idea what to do next. The only clue is a piece of clothing."

Taylor's gut churned. She knew she should have kept some details to herself, but there was no way she could have stopped herself. The chance to find out anything about her sister, after all these years... it was too much. If this is what she suspected… *Oh, God.*

"Come on, then," Garth said. "Let's head down to the beach, and I'll fill you in on my theory."

Taylor and Wesley followed Garth outside. It was mid-morning now, and the sun was still hot, but a cool breeze blew in from the ocean.

They made their way down to the beach, where the ocean stretched before them.

"Listen," Garth began, "you might think this is a missing person's case, but I'm not so convinced. This girl, Amy, was real boy-crazy, by the sounds of it. I think she ran off."

Taylor raised an eyebrow. "Did any young boys on the island go missing with her?"

"Well, no, but—"

"Anything found at the scene that indicated foul play?"

"No—"

"Did any evidence point to her running away?"

"Well, no, but—"

Taylor wrapped up the conversation. "Then it's a missing person's case. End of story. Your problem is that you don't know enough about it, so we're here to help."

Sheriff Garth looked like he was about to have a stroke. "Look, it's my case, and I say it's to be considered a runaway."

"If you say so," Taylor said breezily, wondering why Sheriff Garth was being so difficult about this. She still didn't trust him. "Where did you find the clothing?"

Garth led them down to the beach and over to where a police officer was standing in the sand, near the tree line.

"You found it just over there," Wesley said, pointing.

"Yes," Garth said. "Officer Thompson found it at around nine in the morning yesterday. It's the only trace left of Amy Schuler." Garth paused. "Look, here's the thing. You might think the runaway theory is bullshit, but hear me out. The girl had just turned eighteen. It's not uncommon for girls to take off to escape their lives. Especially here."

Fair enough. It wasn't out of the realm of possibility that a girl like Amy might have run away to escape her life. But Taylor had her doubts. The way Officer Brady had described her, and now Garth, too… it just didn't make sense.

But if this was connected to Angie, Taylor would do everything she could to find her, even if it meant putting her professional life on the line. She didn't care if she was being too persistent.

"What was the clothing?" Taylor asked.

Garth glanced around, as though looking for backup, but no one was there.

"It was her sweatshirt, right?" Taylor asked.

The sheriff nodded. "We got confirmation from the mainland that DNA matched. It's Amy's."

Taylor could feel her heart pounding. She swallowed hard and forced herself to stay calm.

"And do you have any photos of Amy? A file on her?"

"A file, not so much, as there isn't much to say about an eighteen-year-old girl. I know she was the loner type. We're still working on getting more information about who she is from her parents. But I have a photo."

Garth took out his cell phone. He was an older man, and he looked awkward navigating it with his index finger. But he pulled up a photo and showed Taylor and Wesley.

Taylor's stomach bottomed out.

The girl in the photo, Amy…

She looked like Angie.

Taylor felt like a tidal wave was washing over her, and Wesley seemed to notice. “You okay, Sage?” he asked.

She drew a breath. Okay? Not so much. This was huge. She’d suspected it could have something to do with Angie, but this seemed to confirm it. Taylor didn’t want to jump the gun, but in this case, how could she not?

“I’m fine,” Taylor eventually said. “But we need to know more about Amy.” She met Wesley’s eyes. “Let’s talk to her parents.”

CHAPTER SEVEN

Taylor knocked on the beach house door with Wesley at her side. A ball of nerves formed inside Taylor. This beach house was so much like the one her family had rented when she was young. Sand spread throughout the wooden deck, hot in the morning sun, and various plants and weeds grew through the cracks. There was a wooden sailboat hanging from the door.

Moments later, a couple warily answered the door. This was the missing girl's parents.

The woman had short, brown hair with a few streaks of gray; her face was drawn, and her eyes were teary. The man was tall and stout, with dark gray hair. On his face was a very worried look. But his eyes—they were blue-gray. Just like Angie's. Taylor couldn't help but feel sorry for them, but at the same time, the detail that Amy looked similar to what Angie looked like when she disappeared was making Taylor's head spin.

"Mrs. Schuler, Mr. Schuler," Taylor began, "I'm Special Agent Taylor Sage and this is my partner, Special Agent Wesley. We're with the FBI."

"I'm Sherry, Amy's mother, and this is my husband, Evan. Please, come in." Sherry moved to the side to allow them entry.

"Thank you." Taylor and Wesley walked into the house and were greeted by the smell of coffee. The Schulers motioned for them to have a seat at their dining room table.

"This is such a nightmare..." Sherry said, resting her head against her husband's shoulder. Her voice was soft and raspy; it was apparent she had been crying for a long time.

Taylor's mind was reeling. She took note of the details of the house. The furniture was dark oak, the couch and loveseat had a small pillow and blanket on them, like someone was always lying down. On the cabinet, there were some pictures of Amy. Amy as a child, smiling toothily. Amy in high school. Amy on a horse. It seemed she was their only child, as there were no other photos. In every picture, Amy looked like a normal, happy little girl, full of life and laughter. And even her child self looked like Angie. Taylor had to look away; it brought back too many memories.

"We have no idea where Amy is or if she'll ever come back," Sherry said. "It's just so…awful." Her husband rubbed her back.

"I know," Taylor answered, "we just want some answers."

"Of course," Sherry said, "you said you're with the FBI? Do you really think you can help us?"

"I hope so, Mrs. Schuler," Wesley replied, "we actually have a lot of experience with this sort of case. The first step is to try and piece together what happened."

"I'll tell you what happened," Evan cut in. "Our daughter is probably in Mexico by now."

Taylor lifted an eyebrow. "Mexico?"

Sherry sighed. "Forgive my husband. He's being dramatic. But we're fairly sure Amy ran away."

Taylor frowned. It seemed like they were siding with the sheriff's theory. But Taylor didn't buy it. "Has Amy ever run away before?"

"No," Sherry said, "but she has been acting out. A few weeks ago, she had a boyfriend that she snuck out to meet."

"What do you know about this boyfriend?" Wesley asked.

"Not much," Evan replied, "he was a townie. We didn't like him. He was a bad influence on Amy."

"We're sure our daughter is fine," Sherry cut in.

"She just…we think she just needs to get away for a little bit," Evan said.

"You think she'll come back?" Taylor asked.

"I hope so," Evan replied, "but I doubt it."

Taylor frowned. She didn't like what she was hearing. "Do you have any idea where she might have gone?"

"Not at all. She was just boy crazy. She would go with the first boy who'd ask her out." Sherry began to cry again.

Taylor couldn't help but feel frustrated. Until it was proven that Amy had run away, this should have been treated with care. She didn't want to scare the girl's parents, but Taylor pulled a small notepad from her pocket. She opened it and clicked her pen, letting it hover above the paper for a moment before writing down the date. "When was the last time you saw Amy?"

"Two nights ago," Evan said. "She went to bed after dinner."

Taylor flipped the page. "And how long had she been acting out?"

"Just a few weeks," Sherry said. "I was so afraid when she was dating that boy, Dave, but I told myself she was just going through a phase. I should have been more involved."

"You couldn't have known it would lead to this." Evan rubbed her shoulders.

Taylor couldn't help but feel a pang in her heart. It was a parent's job to protect their child; if anything happened, you couldn't forgive yourself.

"You mentioned Amy has a boyfriend?" Wesley asked.

"Not a boyfriend," Sherry said, "but there was a boy she kept bringing up. She was seeing him. She wouldn't tell us much about him, just mentioned she had a crush on that Dave Fisher boy. We forbade her from seeing him. That's why we think she ran away. To punish us."

"But none of the boys on the island have gone missing," Taylor said. "That doesn't strike you as worrying?"

"It surely does," Evan said, "but she's a teenager. Just because she's not with her friends doesn't mean she's missing. Even if she did run away, we're sure she'll contact us soon."

Taylor looked to Wesley, who nodded slightly. They were both thinking the same thing—that was highly unlikely.

"Of course," Taylor said, "we'll want to look at Amy's room, if that's all right. Maybe we can find out more about her mindset before she went missing."

"Sure," Evan replied, "but please, be careful with it. She's a girl. Her room will be…"

"Messy?" Taylor asked.

"Exactly."

"I have a daughter too," Wesley told them. "We'll be as careful as we can."

"Thank you. This way." Evan led them down a long hall that led to a staircase. The walls were covered in pictures of Amy. Staring out of a car window. At the beach. Amy in her school uniform. She was really beautiful, Taylor thought, just like Angie.

Amy's room was larger than Taylor would have expected, but it was filled with photo frames and candles. The bed was covered in stuffed animals and plush dolls. On the wall above her bed, there was a big mirror. Her bedspread was a bright pink; Taylor couldn't help but think of her own room when she was young. And Angie's. Her eyes were drawn to a shelf above the bed. There were small dolls lined up. The doll in front was pushed back slightly, and as she pushed it forward, she noticed that something on the back was missing. Taylor bent down to take a closer look. She brushed her fingers across the shelf, and found a small piece of plastic. She took it and looked around the room. There was nothing else out of the ordinary.

She went to Amy's desk. Maybe there would be a journal or something.

She rifled through the papers on the desk, but found nothing. She opened the drawers, but again, she found nothing. "She kept a diary, didn't she?"

"I'm not sure. If she did, it was private. She wouldn't let us—" Sherry cut off when she saw Taylor lift a scrapbook from the bottom drawer. "That could be it. I don't want you to read it. It's private."

"I think it's just a scrapbook," Taylor said. She could tell by the thick laminated pages. "Do you mind? It might help point us in the right direction."

Hesitantly, Sherry nodded.

Taylor started flipping through it. There were pictures of bathing suit-clad boys and girls, and her and her friends, laughing and smiling. Taylor couldn't help but smile at a few of the pictures. Angie had been that girl. A social butterfly. She flipped a few pages and stopped. There was a doodle of a girl and a boy holding hands. And kissing. The boy wore swim trunks with a flame pattern on them. This must have been Dave Fisher. Taylor took a quick picture with her phone.

Then she flipped through more pages. They were filled with doodles and notes. She stopped again; there was a picture of Amy on the beach. But something didn't look right. It was too dark. She flipped it over. She hadn't noticed it before, but now it was clear. The picture was taken at night. On a night just like the night Taylor and Angie had walked across this same beach. Taylor took another picture with her phone.

"Is everything alright?" Evan asked.

"Yes," Taylor said, snapping out of it. She looked around the room; Sherry and Evan were watching cautiously while Wesley stood with his hands in his pockets, clearly having not found anything important.

"That's all for now," Taylor said. "We'll call you if something comes up."

The parents walked Taylor and Wesley to the foyer, where they thanked them again for their time. With that, Taylor and Wesley left, into the dry and hot morning. They exited the shade of a tree until they were standing under the sun.

"I don't know about this, Sage," Wesley said. "What if she did just run away?"

"What?" Taylor couldn't believe what she was hearing. This was a girl's life on the line. She expected more from Wesley.

"Hey, don't chew my head off," Wesley said. "It's just that we don't have any evidence she didn't run away, either."

Taylor tried not to take it personally, but it reminded her that when Angie went missing, there were some people who theorized she was a runaway as well. But Taylor had never even considered that until the other night, and even then, she'd dismissed the thought. It just wasn't possible. Angie would never do that.

Taylor began walking—she didn't know how to explain this. Wesley sighed and caught up.

"Sorry, Sage," he said, "I just don't know what we're doing here. This isn't our case."

Taylor clammed up. She couldn't tell him the truth. That this could be the same man who took her sister twenty years ago. It was ludicrous, even to Taylor.

But her gut feelings had led her down the right paths before. She couldn't give up. If there was a hope of bringing Amy—and Angie—home, then Taylor had to keep working.

Wesley stopped walking, and Taylor turned back to face him. "What's so personal about this to you?" he asked.

A sinking feeling washed over her. She still hadn't told Wesley the truth. She couldn't bring herself to tell him. It was too personal. The only person Taylor had ever really opened her heart to was Ben, and that had turned out horribly. The idea of Wesley knowing about her life made her feel uneasy. Wesley was a good guy, but still. Taylor didn't open up easy.

But she owed him at least somewhat of an explanation.

"I know it's confusing," she said. "But I need you to just… trust me on this one."

With a sigh, Wesley nodded. "I'm following your lead."

Taylor smiled, tight-lipped, then kept walking. "Good. I think we need to know more about this Dave." Taylor took out her phone and dialed the sheriff's number. He picked up within a few rings.

"Special Agent Sage," he said, "what going on?"

"Do you know anything about Dave Fisher?"

"As a matter of fact, I do," Garth said. "We heard he was seeing Amy, so we talked to him about where he was that night. He's clean.

Was with his friends playing beach volleyball. Lots of witnesses. I don't think the kid did anything."

Damn. "Okay, thanks." Taylor hung up and relayed the information back to Wesley, who just nodded, seemingly in his own world.

"Damn," Wesley said. "Well, that's a dead end."

"Yeah," Taylor said, "but something's going on here, and we need to find out what."

CHAPTER EIGHT

"Two Americanos, black," Wesley told the cashier at the coffee shop, the smell of roasting espresso surrounding him, and he breathed the rich aroma deeply into his lungs. The girl punched in his order, and he glanced over his shoulder at Taylor, who was sitting at a table, on her phone. Her brows were pinched, and she tucked a strand of her black hair over her ear.

Taylor was sitting at a table reading over her notes. She looked stressed, more stressed than he'd ever seen her. Wesley felt Taylor's eyes on him, so he looked away. Off to Wesley's left, a group of girls were sitting at a table, gossiping and sipping coffee.

Taylor had been acting weird since they got here, and Wesley was beginning to grow seriously suspicious about Taylor's motives on this case. She'd asked him to trust her, and in a way, he did—but at the same time, he knew there were things she was hiding from him. He wondered what it was that she wasn't telling him and why it was so important that she felt she needed to lie to her partner about it.

He glanced over his shoulder at Taylor again as he waited for his coffee. She was on her phone, tilting her head away from him ever so slightly. A strand of black hair fell down in front of her face, and she tucked it behind her ear with a dark tendril still falling down beside her nose.

He was gonna need to start getting some answers soon.

They'd stopped at this touristy, hipster café for some coffee, but it was nearly ten a.m. now and Wesley hadn't seen Taylor eat anything. He was getting hungry himself. Taylor would probably resist, but it wouldn't kill them to take fifteen and grab a bite to eat.

"Add a couple bagels on there," Wesley muttered to the cashier.

"Coming right up," the girl, a teenager with piercings, said.

Wesley paid for the coffee and food, then moved over to the other side of the counter to wait it out.

When he looked over his shoulder again, Taylor was talking to somebody—two teenage girls. Probably interrogating them to see what they knew about Amy.

Wesley glanced over at the employees behind the counter. They were still making the order. He had time to call in a quick favor while Taylor was occupied. If Taylor wasn't going to tell him the truth, then he'd find it out himself.

Taking out his phone, Wesley dialed an old friend at the FBI—Special Agent Serge Ray. Wesley had worked with Serge years ago, even before his leave after the incident in his twenties, where he'd been forced to shoot another undercover cop to keep up his character. In some ways, Serge was like a father figure to Wesley, which he appreciated since he'd never really had a father of his own.

That was why Wesley was there for Maisie unequivocally. He'd never be a deadbeat, not like his dad. Although he did wish he was home more to spend time with her, Maisie was a smart girl and he knew she understood that everything he did, he did for her. One day, his FBI salary would pay for her education.

Serge picked up within a few rings.

"Wes, that really you?" Serge's grizzled voice came through the phone.

"Hey, Serge," Wesley said, turning away and keeping quiet. Taylor was still talking to the teenagers across the café. "How's it going, buddy? I wanted to know if you could look into someone for me real quick."

"You got it, man. Why are you whispering? Secret op?"

"You could say that. It's actually about my new partner at Quantico. Special Agent Taylor Sage."

Serge paused. "I've heard about her. What do you wanna know? I don't know her personally, but I could do some quick recon."

"Thanks. I'm working a case with her right now, a little off the books. A missing girl over on Brock Island. But I'm not so sure this girl's really missing. Sage is convinced she is, but not only that—she's taking it all real personal. She's hiding something, and she's a tough nut to crack. Was wondering if you could dig anything up real quick."

"Give me a minute."

Silence took over. Wesley smiled at an employee who handed him the two coffees. He nodded and waited for the bagels. Taylor was still talking to the two girls—Wesley could only assume she was digging up information on Amy Schuler. Part of him felt like a dick for spying on her like this, but at the same time, spying was his job. If Taylor was going to rope him into a case like this, he at least needed some idea of what he was getting himself into.

Finally, Serge came through with an answer.

"Does the name Angie Sage mean anything to you?"

Wesley paused. He'd never heard Taylor mention anything about any Angie.

"No," Wesley said. "What's the deal there?"

"You said she's getting personal on a missing persons case, yeah? Well, get this. Two decades ago, one Angela "Angie" Sage, sixteen, went missing without a trace. She left behind her sister, Taylor, and her parents, Randall and Linda. I don't know about you, but I sort of doubt this is a coincidence."

Damn. Now Wesley did feel bad about digging.

Taylor was so invested in this case because her own sister had gone missing. But that was two decades ago. Not exactly a short time. Surely Taylor didn't think they were connected. That'd be nuts.

"Thanks, Serge. I appreciate it." Wesley hung up. He wanted to tell Serge to keep his information on Taylor to himself, but it was too late. Besides, Serge was an agent. He could keep quiet—if he wanted to.

Wesley had no reason to mistrust Taylor, at least, not anymore. He had his own secrets in his past, just like she was keeping something from him, and he had to live with that. Even though Serge had dug up information about Taylor, it didn't mean she was keeping secrets from him. Not really. Serge had just uncovered some bad memories.

Maybe Taylor was seeing her own missing sister in Amy Schuler. Maybe she felt obligated to help. Wesley couldn't gripe her for that, although he did wonder if they were doing this the right way.

We should call this in, tell Winchester what we're up to...

But maybe there was another reason Taylor wanted to keep this off the books. Wesley decided to hold back on calling it in for now and see where this led.

Finally, an employee slid two plates with bagels on them at Wesley. "Sorry for the wait—our toaster is a little busted."

"Thanks," Wesley muttered, just as he looked over to see Taylor approaching him.

"Here, let me help with that." She grabbed the two coffees, then eyed the bagels. "You got food too?"

Wesley averted his eyes. "Wouldn't kill us to eat, Sage."

"Right. I know. It's just—" Taylor frowned, looking down at the bagels. "I'm not hungry. But we should talk about the case, anyway."

Wesley shrugged, then grabbed his bagels.

They went and sat at a table by the window. Wesley noted the girls Taylor had been talking to before were gone. They sat across from each other, and Wesley took a sip of his black coffee, then a bite of his bagel with cream cheese.

"What was up with the girls?" Wesley asked.

Taylor's eyes flashed on his. "They knew Amy."

Wesley slowly chewed. "And?"

"And..." Taylor took a breath. "They named someone who they think had a thing for her. He's a nineteen-year-old named Ryan Jones. Apparently, he had a thing for Amy, but she didn't feel the same way because she liked that guy named Dave."

"Hot lead," Wesley muttered.

"It's not conclusive, but it's something," Taylor said, biting her lip. "I think we should speak with him."

Wesley paused. He did agree. But if they were going to go this far, go around questioning witnesses, then they should probably let HQ know.

"Hold on there," Wesley said. "Not so fast."

Taylor's eyes hardened. "You think I'm wrong?"

"I didn't say that," Wesley said. "I think we should bring this to Winchester before we do anything. We're working a case off the books, Sage. That's not exactly professional. What are we messing around here for?"

"I think this is important," Taylor said. "And by the way—we're not messing around. I'm doing this because it's my job. I'm always an agent, whether I'm on the books or not."

"I know. You're just not thinking this through. Right now, this is the local police's job."

"Look, Wes, I'm really glad you came, but if you don't want to be here then—"

"I'm just trying to do my job," Wesley said. "And so should you. Which means not getting in over your head.". If you think I'm gonna let you do it alone, you're wrong. I'm still on your side here, Sage. But I need to know the truth. What are we really doing here?"

He waited for Taylor to tell the truth. To fess up about this missing sister, Angie.

But she didn't. She said, "Wesley, I told you. I just happened upon this case and I want to help. Are you really okay with leaving a missing girl's life in the hands of local police who don't even believe she's missing? You have a daughter. Think about that."

Wesley felt a flare of anger. "Don't bring my daughter into this, Sage."

Taylor looked down at the bagel she still hadn't touched. "I'm sorry. I just felt like you, of all people, should care."

"I do care." And he did. He was just feeling extremely worried about where this could be going.

"I'm sorry," Taylor said, looking him in the eye. "It's just... it's been a while since anyone cared."

Wesley studied her. She was telling the truth, at least about that. She hadn't been able to save her sister Angie then, but now she felt like she could save Amy. "I don't doubt you care," Wesley said. "I'm just not sure how you're getting so invested in this case."

He watched her face, waiting for an answer. But it didn't look like Taylor was going to come clean anytime soon.

She stood up and picked up her bagel, taking a bite. "Let's take this to go."

He watched her go, then sighed and grabbed a napkin. He wiped his mouth clean and got up to leave, leaving his half-eaten bagel behind.

Wesley knew Taylor was a good agent. She'd proved that before, but this time, things were different. She was getting personal.

If she was doing this case to help make herself feel better about her missing sister, or to help her deal with some sort of guilt over the fact that she hadn't saved her, well, there was nothing Wesley could do. He'd tried to talk to her, but she wasn't having it.

He looked outside the window to see her standing there, waiting for him. She didn't look angry. She just looked... distant. Probably thinking about Angie.

And he couldn't help but wonder if that'd cloud her judgement.

He didn't want to think about it. He still wanted to believe in Taylor, even though he couldn't make himself believe that he'd been wrong about her. He just hoped that Taylor was able to keep her feelings in check. He didn't want to see her get hurt.

If he had to, he would call this whole thing off.

Because Taylor Sage was getting too close to the case.

And that was a dangerous place to be.

CHAPTER NINE

With Wesley at her side, Taylor approached the beach house that Ryan Jones was allegedly staying at. The girls at the coffee shop had given her good intel; apparently, Ryan was obsessed with Amy, even though she had an obvious fling with his friend, Dave. Ryan was really jealous, and according to the girls, he'd lashed out at Amy when drunk a few times.

The beach house was painted yellow and glowed in the late-morning sun. The color was bright and warm. The rays of the sun bounced off the walls and windows in little explosions of light. The sounds of waves crashing against the beach on the other side of the dune filled the air with an incessant rhythm that was a part of every breath Taylor took.

They'd wasted more time than she would have liked at the coffee shop, but Wesley had been persistent. While Taylor was interviewing the girls, she swore she'd seen him on the phone, talking to somebody. But she wasn't one hundred percent sure. Right now, all Taylor cared about was finding Amy Schuler.

If that ended up giving a clue about what happened to Angie, then that would be the icing on the cake.

As they neared the beach house, Taylor made out a group of boys playing beach volleyball. The girl in the shop had shown Taylor a picture of Ryan. He was the tall, lithe one with the curly blonde hair. It was time to ask him some questions.

"What if he doesn't know anything?" Wesley asked.

Taylor turned to give him a look. "What do you mean?"

"What if he's just a teenager who got in over his head with a girl and now she's gone? Then what are we supposed to do?"

"That's a lot of 'what ifs,' Wes."

"I know," Wesley said. "I'm just saying that we have a lot of different possibilities here."

"We'll deal with it when we get there," Taylor said, walking forward and approaching the volleyball players. Wesley followed, looking around in the daylight.

She wasn't sure what it was, but Wesley was just really gun-shy about her intentions. Taylor knew that he was concerned about her, but he had a way of making her feel like she was doing something wrong. Like he could see through the real reasons Taylor had come to this island.

The boys on the beach stopped what they were doing when they saw the two FBI agents. Wesley and Taylor approached them slowly, not wanting to spook anybody.

Ryan took a step back when he saw Taylor. He looked like he was in his late teens, with high cheekbones and a lean, shirtless body. "What's going on?"

Taylor flashed her badge. She saw that Wesley had his out too. "We're looking for Ryan Jones?"

"That's me," Ryan said. "What's this about?"

Taylor saw three other boys standing there, looking just as confused as Ryan was. "Is there somewhere we can talk?"

Ryan's eyes darted back and forth. He seemed nervous.

"I... I don't think we've done anything wrong," he said.

"You haven't," Taylor said. "But it would be best if we could go somewhere and talk in private."

Ryan's Adam's apple bobbed as he swallowed, and he nodded and turned to the other boys. "You guys go on ahead—I'll catch up."

"Hey, man," one of them said, and Taylor couldn't tell if he was annoyed or just worried. "You want some company?"

"Nah, I'm cool. Just... don't go too far," Ryan said. "I'll be right back, I promise."

The boys shrugged and retreated to the house. Wesley and Taylor followed Ryan, who sat down on a sand dune and looked out at the ocean. Taylor could feel the breeze off the sea, filled with salt and brine.

"So, Ryan," Taylor began. "What do you think this is about?"

"I don't know, I... I don't think I want to talk to you."

Wesley stepped forward. "I think you'd better talk to her. It's about Amy Schuler."

Ryan's eyes got wide. "Amy?"

"Yeah," Taylor said. "We're looking for her."

"I don't... I don't know where she is. I haven't seen her in a couple days."

"Are you sure about that, Ryan?" Wesley pressed. "I hope you wouldn't hide something from the FBI. That could land you in a lot of trouble."

Taylor shot him a grateful smile. Wesley's intimidation factor could be good sometimes, especially when dealing with male perps. Taylor had learned that well on their last case. And she was grateful that despite his misgivings, Wesley was still on her side, and still helping. She wouldn't forget this.

Ryan rubbed the back of his neck. "No, I'm serious. I was worried about her, but I haven't seen her, I swear."

Taylor frowned. "What were you worried about?"

"I don't know. I just knew that she was going out with Dave a lot. And whenever she'd go out with him..." Ryan trailed off. He clenched his fists in the sand.

There it was. That angry jealousy that the girl in the café had told Taylor about.

Ryan was acting like a nice guy, but Taylor was starting to see through it.

It was incredible what people would do to hide their true selves. Taylor had experience with that firsthand. Sometimes in her life, she'd wondered if being an open book would help her out, but it just wasn't in her nature.

It had been in Angie's, though.

"What would happen?" Taylor asked.

"Nothing," Ryan said. "That's the issue. Dave didn't even really seem to like her. They never kissed or anything. I just felt like Amy was wasting her time on him."

"Maybe there was some jealousy there?" Taylor lightly prodded.

"What?" Ryan scowled. "No. I wasn't jealous."

"I think you were," Wesley said. "I think you're lying through your teeth."

Ryan whipped his head around. He looked like he was about to get up, but Taylor stepped forward, blocking his path. Wesley glared at Ryan. "You better watch yourself, kid. I'm going to find out if you know anything or not."

"What—what the hell is your problem?" Ryan asked.

The hostility was quickly rising. Taylor turned back to Ryan. "Okay, so tell me about Amy, then. If you weren't jealous, why did you care if Amy had a crush on Dave?"

Ryan looked at Taylor like she was being ridiculous. "I liked her. Amy was a great girl."

"Was?" Taylor asked.

Still sitting in the sand, Ryan pulled his knees to his chest and hid the bottom part of his face. He was acting weird. Closed off. Taylor didn't trust it.

"I mean, is..." He shook his head. "It doesn't matter, okay? Amy would never like me now anyway."

"And why is that?" Taylor pressed.

Ryan let out a sigh. "Okay. You can't tell anyone this—it'll ruin my life, but..."

Taylor lifted an eyebrow. Where was this going?

"There's this girl, Marcy," Ryan said. "She's dating my friend, Greg. Marcy is Amy's best friend. And after Amy rejected me for the millionth time, I sort of..." He took a deep breath. "I started hooking up with Marcy. I didn't want Amy to know because then she'd never like me, and Greg would kick my ass."

Typical teenage drama, Taylor thought. In those years, it seems like almost everyone is out to betray.

"So were you ever going to tell Amy?" Taylor asked.

"No." Ryan looked up at her. "I'm an idiot, okay? I'm a real asshole. I never wanted her to find out. I never thought about anything except for how to make myself look cool and how to keep Greg from beating the crap out of me. I was a coward. And now Amy is gone, and Marcy hates me, and I just know that Amy hates me too."

Taylor could see tears welling up in Ryan's eyes. His mouth was downturned in a frown, like the weight of everything was too much for him to bear.

"So that's it," he said, shaking his head. "I don't know where she is."

As much as Taylor didn't want to admit it, Ryan was not looking like much of a dastardly kidnapper.

And if she was being honest with herself...

She didn't *want* him to be the kidnapper.

Because Ryan was only nineteen. Which meant he was born one year after Angie went missing. There wasn't a chance in hell he could have had anything to do with her disappearance.

It wasn't that Taylor didn't care about Amy—she did. But she also hoped, desperately, that this could lead her to Angie. After the symbols, the dreams... it all had to mean something.

She couldn't just leave it alone, especially not when there was a lead.

Besides, what if Ryan was telling the truth, and he really didn't know anything?

Taylor sighed. "Okay. We believe you. For now. But if you know anything, you better tell us."

Ryan nodded. "I got it."

"Good." Taylor turned to Wesley. "Come on. Let's go."

Wesley wordlessly followed her. They found themselves moving across a sand dune, their feet swishing across the sand.

"What do you think?" Taylor asked as they walked off.

"He seems innocent," Wesley said. "You gave up on him pretty quick."

"Yeah, well..." Taylor stuffed her hands in her pockets. The black fabric was hot against her skin, especially under the sun, but the breeze from the ocean was cool. "I just don't think he's our guy."

Wesley nodded. "Well, let's not waste any more time."

Taylor nodded. "You're right. We should head to the station and see if those cops have figured anything else out." She turned and started walking.

"Hey."

She turned around and faced Wesley. He had his arms crossed over his broad chest.

"What?" Taylor asked.

"I know you don't like me very much," Wesley said. "And I know you think I'm some sort of jackass. But I know you're passionate about this case, and I'm passionate about it too. And I just want to make sure you know that I'm going to do everything I can to help you."

Taylor was taken aback. "What makes you think I don't like you, Wes?"

"My methods aren't like yours, and we've barely worked together."

True, Taylor had gotten frustrated with Wesley on their last case, but this was different. She'd built trust in him. She wouldn't have called him here to help her if she didn't have faith.

Taylor sighed. "Wesley, I called you here because we worked so well together last time, and I do trust you."

"You're a hard woman to please," Wesley said.

Taylor was about to roll her eyes, but she stopped herself. She had to admit, Wesley was right. She wasn't the easiest person to work with, and she'd burned some bridges with some of her coworkers and friends before.

Maybe she was coming on too strong, too soon. It was more of a risk than she was willing to take. She had to remind herself that this was about saving lives, not about making friends. "I know I have a... reputation. I'm not always easy to work with."

Wesley shrugged. "I know you have this fierce determination that makes you a damn good agent. That's your reputation, Sage."

Taylor was taken aback. From what she'd seen, it wasn't like Wesley to get all sentimental. She wasn't sure what his angle was here, although she appreciated him respecting her work. "Thanks, but what's with the compliments?"

Wesley paused, thinking on it. "I just wanted you to know that I respect you as an agent. And you can trust me."

"I do, Wes."

Wesley looked like he wanted to say something more. He opened his mouth a couple times, but then he just turned away, apparently deciding against whatever he was about to say.

"Come on," Taylor said, and they started walking again.

CHAPTER TEN

He entered the soundproofed room and closed the door behind him, trapping out the rest of the world. What he had in here was for his eyes only. The rest couldn't see. He took her in and smiled.

This girl was his prettiest catch yet.

That long hair, those blue eyes so light they were almost gray.

Just looking at her made his stomach roll in the best way.

She struggled against the restraints in the chair. The fishing line he'd used to tie her with pressed against her peachy skin.

Oh, this was going to be delicious.

Her eyes went wide and her mouth opened in a silent and fruitless plea. She let out a whimper. She had already wasted all her energy screaming, but she knew now that it was pointless. No one could hear her in here. He kept the smile on his face as he slowly walked up to her.

"No need to be afraid," he coaxed. "We're just going to have a little fun."

Her eyes darted right and left, searching for a way out. She was out of luck. There was no escape.

"I want you to take a look at this," he said.

He held up the camera and turned it on. The image on the screen was grainy and small, but the moment she saw it, she knew. He could see it in her eyes. It was a picture of her, three nights ago, with some boy her age. Some pathetic little boy who could never please her like he could.

Foolish girl. He knew he was too old for her. He wouldn't be her choice. But she was his. He would show her why that pathetic boy would never be good enough.

"I'm going to make you a deal," he said. "A choice. You can love him, or you can love me."

He looked at her, feeling his eyes sting. So many memories came flooding back. *Patricia.* The first time she cheated, the first time she broke his heart. It was with some other guy, a younger guy, a pathetic guy. *But she loved me,* he told himself. *She told me she loved me.*

He needed to hear it again, one more time.

"Make the right choice," he murmured.

She let out a soft and ragged sob.

"I want to hear you say it."

She was a mess. She was shaking, tears streaming down her face and a long line of drool running down her chin. He frowned and grabbed the tendril of spit. He wiped it against her face and smeared it across her cheek.

She was so pretty. He loved the way her skin looked in the dim light.

Beautiful. But her life would become a past event, like the others, if she did not make the right choice.

Tell me you love me, Patricia. Tell me I'm worthy.

"I said, I want you to say it," he said.

He made sure to enunciate each syllable.

"Please, no." She looked at him with pleading eyes. Eyes that stared straight through him and into his soul. Eyes that begged for forgiveness. Eyes that pleaded for his mercy. She struggled against the fishing line, straining against it. Her breathing came in shallow gasps.

"Eyes up," he said.

She looked at him. He could see the hope in her eyes. She could make a deal. For her, it was an act of mercy, but it hurt him.

He smiled again. "I'm not going to hurt you, my dear, but I need you to say it."

She looked at him again. She knew what he was going to ask, and she knew it was the last thing she could offer to save her own life. She sighed.

"Please. Do anything you want to me, but don't kill me," she said.

"I'm a reasonable man." He paced in front of her and took a deep breath, inhaling her scent. It was too different from Patricia's. Patricia had smelled like lavender and lilac. This girl just smelled like the beach.

But she looked so much like his Patricia; she was the closet thing he could have.

"I just want you to say it, Patricia. Say it."

"I'm not Patricia!" she screamed.

He slapped her, hard. She let out a yelp.

"I want to hear you say it," he said.

She was crying again. Whether it was from pain or desperation, he didn't know. He didn't care, either. He wanted her to say it. He put his hand around the back of her head and pulled her in close. "Say. It."

His face was a foot away from hers. He could feel her hot breath on his face. Her beautiful face.

"I'm not Patricia!" she screamed. "I'm Amy! I'm Amy!" Her eyes filled with tears.

He grabbed her face in his hands. "Tell me you love me. Now."

She began to struggle again, her hands grasping at the fishing line. He pulled her face toward him.

"Please. Please. I'm not Patricia. Please. I'm Amy. I'm Amy. Just let me go..."

"SAY IT!" he screamed.

She closed her eyes and swallowed hard, her face turning red. He was going to enjoy this. No matter what she said, he was going to enjoy it.

"I-I love you."

He smiled and let go of her face. He released his grip on her and let her fall. He watched as she struggled to breathe. It was like a miracle. She had a second chance at life.

It was a shame it wouldn't last long.

CHAPTER ELEVEN

Taylor knocked on the door of Brock Island's sheriff's office with Wesley at her side. She opened the door, and Sheriff Garth lifted his head from his papers at his desk, looking as cantankerous as earlier.

"You again," he said.

Taylor stepped into the office, Wesley behind her.

"Yes, we're still here," Taylor said. "I spoke to Amy's parents. They think she ran off too."

"That's because she probably did," Garth said. "I told you before, girls have run away from his island before. Not a lot of teenagers wanna spend their lives here."

"Right, about that," Taylor said. "I'd like to know more about these girls you say are runaways."

"What for?" Garth said. "You're wasting valuable time. Day's wasting. Here's what I'm saying, a lot of teenagers don't want to stay here, so they run away. They're probably in the big cities. They ain't coming back."

"Have you proved that before?" Taylor asked

"Of course I have. Some parents say they get a call from their kid a few weeks later. No problem. I'm sure that's what's going on with Amy Schuler."

Taylor paused, thinking on it. She needed to know more about the others who ran away. "Were any of them ever not found?"

"Maybe one or two," Garth said.

This was frustrating Taylor. The FBI should've been assigned to these cases sooner. Not everyone who went missing was a runaway. Taylor had a pit in her gut, a feeling that was telling her there was more going on here on Brock Island than she'd bargained for. If that were the case, then she intended to find out exactly what was going on.

"Can I see the files on the girls who were never found?" Taylor asked. "I'd like to compare them with Amy's case."

Garth became even more irritated. "I don't see why you'd wanna look at that," he said. "You're only getting in the way."

"I'm getting in the way?" Taylor said.

"That's right. You're out of your jurisdiction. You're not needed. You should be helping with the Schuler case, not the others. Those cases are solved. They're runaways. You're barking up the wrong tree."

"I'll decide whether we're going to look into them or not," Taylor said, annoyed. "If you want to help, then give me the files on the runaways. We can't make a proper investigation if we only have half of the information."

"Damn feds…" Garth stood up from his desk and stepped to the left. He pulled out a file from the shelf and handed it to Taylor. "This is the case file of the last girl who went missing. The girls before her are there too."

"Thank you," Taylor said.

"Don't mention it," Garth said. "Now get out of my hair."

The two FBI agents walked out of the office, closing the door behind them. Normally, Taylor would go to her car to review files like this, but of course, she and Wesley had taken the ferry here. They sat down in the waiting area of the police station. There was no one there, after all, so they had privacy.

"You start with this one," Taylor said, handing Wesley a file.

He grunted, but opened up the manila folder. He looked at the first page, and then handed it to Taylor. "This one's from six months ago."

They both looked through their files, watching the clock on the wall tick down the minutes. The files were skimming over the same things, a lot of the information useless.

One girl was named Jessica Clements. She was the oldest of all of the girls who were never found, and she was only nineteen at the time she went missing. She looked at the picture of Jessica on the front of the file. She was pretty, a brunette with bangs. She was smiling in the picture. Taylor wondered why a girl like that would up and leave.

Looking closer at the photo, something struck her about Jessica. She didn't look like Angie the same way Amy did.

But there were some similarities. The blue-gray eyes and dark hair.

Taylor's pulse jumped. There was still hope this case could be connected to Angie. This could still be the same guy who had her. She tried to keep her excitement in as she glanced at Wesley's file, hoping for similar news.

"What do you have, Wesley?" Taylor asked him.

"Girl reported missing, age eighteen," Wesley muttered.

"Let me see the photo." Taylor needed to know if she looked like Angie too.

The girl in the photo had dark brown hair, similar to Angie's. She had light blue eyes, not exactly gray, but still very light in color. Taylor was worried she was getting her hopes up. She couldn't get too excited.

Wesley looked over the file again.

"This is Brenda Grimmie," he said. "A party girl who was suspected of running off for a boy in another city. Her parents said she'd been talking to a guy online. They never saw her again."

"Did they ever find him?" Taylor asked.

"Nope," Wesley said.

"Let's check out the other case file," Taylor said.

Wesley reluctantly handed Taylor the file.

They skimmed over it.

"This is a file from this year," Wesley said. "Samantha Skelly. A runaway, age eighteen. She's a part of the missing foster care system."

"Why did she run away?" Taylor asked.

"Her file says she's a runaway because her foster parents abused her," Wesley said.

"Where were her parents born?" Taylor asked.

"Her father's from Brock Island and her mother is from Canada," Wesley said. "The file says they don't live here anymore."

Taylor sat back on it. They had at least three girls now who had all left Brock Island, never to be seen again. It all happened over the course of several months, but still; this was enough to tell Taylor it was suspicious.

Taylor stood up. "I think we should pay the parents a visit."

***

Walking across the hot island was growing tiring, and Taylor could tell Wesley was getting fed up. They had found Jessica's parents' address and were on the way to their beach house, but the heat was getting to Taylor too; she found her mind wandering, her focus deteriorating. But she couldn't give up. Not on Amy. Not on Angie.

"There it is," Taylor said.

They passed a few houses, and then finally they were in front of the gate of the Clements' home. The Clements' house sat on a hill, not far from the beach, and was a single-story home. It was white and clean, and had a channel for a weeping willow tree near the front door. It had a welcoming feel attached with the weeping willow. The windows were all lined with curtains. There was a large dock leading to the sea.

Taylor knocked on the door. Jessica's mother opened it moments later and greeted them with a grim look on her face.

“Can I help you?”

"FBI, and we're here about your daughter," Taylor explained. "I was wondering if we could talk."

The women nodded and let the agents into her house. The flooring was polished wood with a red and white checkered pattern. The walls were white, the dressers were a light green, and there was a single window with a view to the ocean from the living room. Mrs. Clements brought them to a cottage-style kitchen.

"Please have a seat," Mrs. Clements said.

Taylor and Wesley sat in the chairs by the table. Mrs. Clements stood in the kitchen and continued her cooking, filling the room with the smell of sizzling onions.

"I hear you're the mother of Jessica Clements," Taylor said.

"I am," she said.

"Do you mind if I ask you a few questions about her?" Taylor asked.

Mrs. Clements turned off the pan and faced Taylor. "I suppose not… although there isn’t much to say that hasn’t already been said.”

“We’re just gathering information,” Taylor told her. "Why did your daughter run away?"

"She said she wanted to find her father," Mrs. Clements said.

"Why, did she not know him?" Taylor asked.

"No, she only knew my husband, who was her stepfather. But her real father was out of the picture."

"Did she ever find him?"

"Not according to him, but Jessica also had a boyfriend she'd been secretly seeing, and I always suspected that was the real reason she left home."

Mrs. Clements was taking things out of the oven and placing them on the table. She was setting two plates down, along with two forks and two water glasses.

"Thank you, Mrs. Clements," Taylor said, “but we don’t need anything.”

Across from Taylor, Wesley stiffened. Maybe she was just speaking for herself. Mrs. Clements stopped her cooking and sat down at the table with Taylor and Wesley.

"So, you didn't know anything about this boyfriend?" Taylor asked.

"No, but I suspected something," Mrs. Clements said. "Jessica was always secretive about where she was going when she left home. She always had a phone, too, but she never let me see the phone or her text messages. And she always arrived home very late at night. It was very suspicious."

"Did you ever confront her about this?" Wesley asked.

"Of course I did," Mrs. Clements said. "I questioned her about her boyfriend, but whenever I asked about where she had been, she would clam up and refuse to talk. Jessica had never shown any interest in meeting her birth father, so her sudden desire to was a red flag to me. She ran away eight months ago, and I haven't heard from her since."

Taylor couldn't believe Mrs. Clements could be so casual about this. How could she know that Jessica really ran away and wasn't kidnapped?

"Are you sure she ran away?" Taylor asked.

"That's what the police told me," Mrs. Clements said.

Taylor paused. She didn't want to ruin this woman's day, but: "Mrs. Clements, what if Jessica didn't run away? What if somebody took her?"

"What?" Her face went pale. "I don't believe that. Really, I would not put it past Jessica to run away. I hope I'll hear from her again."

"I'm sorry to say this, but it's a very strong possibility she didn't run away," Wesley said.

"You're telling me my daughter was kidnapped?" Mrs. Clements asked. "Why would you say that?"

"Because we found three other girls who all ran away from their homes, and they all disappeared," Taylor said. "They were all originally from Brock Island, and we think that maybe, Jessica was also kidnapped."

"Oh my God," she said. She stood up. "Excuse me for a second."

With that, she ran out of the room. Taylor and Wesley sat at the table and waited for Mrs. Clements to return. Wesley let out a sigh and gave Taylor a look.

"What?" she said.

"Are we really helping here?" he asked her.

Taylor felt a jolt of guilt. She could hear Mrs. Clements hyperventilating in the next room. This woman had clearly accepted her daughter's fate, but now she was getting another story, from the FBI at that. Maybe Wesley had a point, but still; in the pursuit of truth, sometimes people had to face difficult realities.

Mrs. Clements came back in, gathering herself.

"I don't understand," she said. "My daughter left home before she was even old enough to legally drink. She was probably with her boyfriend, whoever he is, and they ran away together. We've had nothing but heartache since then. I'm sure it's been the same for the other parents. This kidnapping theory—the police never told me that."

"Did you ever know this boyfriend?" Taylor asked.

"No, like I said, Jessica was secretive, but..."

The realization seemed to wash over Mrs. Clements. After all this time, she was realizing how blind she had been to assume her daughter had run away.

"Oh my God, my Jessica... are you saying she could be hurt?"

"We don't know that," Wesley cut in.

"We're just worried somebody could be taking girls from this island," Taylor clarified.

"But maybe Jessica did run away," Wesley said. "We can't know for sure, Mrs. Clements."

Mrs. Clements's eyes glossed over. "How dare you two come into my house and say all this? I've accepted what happened with my daughter, and now you're reopening all the old wounds."

"I'm sorry, Mrs. Clements," Wesley said.

"No," she said. "I don't want to hear another word."

Taylor nodded and stood up, Wesley following. They'd clearly used up their time here, and it was time to leave.

"We'll be in touch if we find anything," Taylor said.

"You have a nice day, Mrs. Clements," Wesley said, and they left her house.

Once outside again, Taylor felt awful for sticking her nose in this. In her pursuit to find Angie, was she hurting more people than she was helping?

No, she couldn't believe that.

It was unfortunate if Mrs. Clements was hurting now, but Taylor was certain Amy Schuler had not run away. And if the same person who took Jessica, also took Amy, then Taylor needed to do what was necessary to find out the truth.

"Maybe this whole thing is just a coincidence," Wesley said as they walked.

"I don't think so," Taylor said.

"Taylor, this is getting really serious. I know this is hard for you to hear, but we might just be overreacting," Wesley said.

"No, I think we're right about this," Taylor said. "Jessica and Amy were kidnapped. If we can find who took them, then we will know for sure. The only way to do that is to find out more."

"I have a bad feeling about this," Wesley said.

"Me too."

There was another thing itching at the back of Taylor's mind. And that was the fact that yes, they had several missing girls—four, in fact. Jessica, Brenda, Samantha, and now Amy. All eighteen, or around that age, as Jessica was a year older.

Another thing Taylor remembered from the file was that all the girls seemed to disappear from the beach at night. A few witnesses had reported seeing them near the water alone before they were reported missing. And that lined up with what happened to Amy, too.

They were dealing with a kidnapper. Taylor was certain of it.

But that left one haunting question for Taylor to ask:

Where are the girls now?

CHAPTER TWELVE

Wesley felt like he was in over his head.

As he followed Taylor through town, he was getting hot and sweaty beneath his shirt—and more than a little frustrated with his partner. She'd had plenty of opportunities to come clean about her sister, and Wesley was starting to believe she never would.

They'd spent the morning asking more about the disappearances. Even talked to a friend of Jessica Clements, who also bought the story that Jessica had run off. It was after noon now. They'd crossed the threshold from the residential neighborhood to downtown, and Wesley's stomach was roaring with hunger. He wanted to take a break.

The warm air shimmered over the sidewalk. It smelled like burning rubber in places and like the fumes from a skunk being run down by a car in others. There were storefronts on one side and rows of houses on the other, most decorated with American flags or fresh spring flowers or hand-painted signs: *Welcome Home, son*! and *Welcome Home, girl!* and *Welcome Home, soldier!*

A rickety food cart with a metal roof shaded by striped umbrellas sat in front of an open-air store that sold cards and commemorative plates edged with gold leaf. An elderly man behind the counter waved at them, and Wesley nodded back.

"Sage," Wesley said, catching up to her, "I need to stop for lunch."

“You go ahead,” Taylor said. “I can catch up.”

Wesley planted his feet on the sidewalk and watched Taylor pace ahead, toward the police station. But he wasn't budging. Not until he got some answers.

Wesley had been more than patient, waiting for Taylor to tell the truth about why they were here. This wasn't just a case for her. She was clearly invested because her own sister had gone missing years ago. The truth was, Wesley was getting worried about her. This wasn’t the Taylor Sage he knew.

Maybe it was time to just call this into Winchester behind Sage's back.

But if he did that, she'd never trust him again, and Wesley could tell Taylor didn't give her trust away easily.

To hell with it, he thought. He was done waiting around; it was time to demand answers.

"Sage, hold on."

She stopped and turned, her face clouded with annoyance. “Everything okay?”

Wesley shook his head. He wasn't going to play this game with her. "First of all, I want to know why we're really here on this island. You've been holding out on me."

"No, I haven't," she deflected.

"I also want to know about your sister," he said.

Taylor’s eyes flashed. “I’m sorry—what?”

He held his ground. “You heard what I said, Sage.”

The look on Taylor's face told Wesley already he was right. She'd been holding out on him. Taylor's face crumpled, and she turned away from him.

"What's going on?" Wesley asked. "Why do you have to make this so hard for me? Just tell me the truth.”

"I'm not making it hard for you," she said.

Silence befell them. Taylor wrapped her arms over her chest and looked down, clearly upset.

"I'm sorry, I shouldn't have lied to you," she said. "But I just didn't want you to know."

Wesley stood there by himself on the sidewalk. He uncrossed his arms and took a step toward her. "To know what?" he asked.

"I'm sorry I didn't tell you before," Taylor said, her voice faltering. Wesley felt bad for her, but he was tired of having to play a guessing game with her.

"Just come out with it, Sage. Why is this case so personal to you?"

Taylor drew a breath, then: "Two decades ago, my sister, Angie, went missing without a trace. All that was left behind was a shred of clothing."

Finally, she'd come clean. Wesley nodded. "Sage, I'd already figured that out."

Her eyes snapped to his. "Yeah, I sort of put two and two together.”

"I'm sorry, but I looked into you a bit." Wesley ran his hand over his face. "I had to know what you were hiding from me."

Taylor wore a stunned expression. “I should’ve known you’d do that.”

"I mean, you're not the only one who's still hurting from something that happened long ago,” Wesley said.

The truth was that he had his own demon far out in his past. He wasn't squeaky clean by any means. He'd grown up with a single mom who traded new boyfriends in like they were pairs of shoes, and those boyfriends were not exactly good guys. Wesley's real dad was a deadbeat, of course, and he'd never met him. Never looked for him either; he didn't care. But those guys his mom would bring home were bad news, always getting his mom hooked on cocaine, always bringing guns in the house.

That was where Wesley's original fascination with becoming an officer came from. When he was a kid, he used to imagine himself growing big and taking down bad guys like his mom's boyfriends. They'd beat him up and throw him around, and he'd think that someday, no one would ever throw him around again.

Of course, Wesley had chosen the FBI over police work, but he much preferred things this way. Still, he understood Taylor; he knew that the past shapes everything in the future.

As they met each other's eyes, the truth dawned on both of them at once.

"We're not so different, are we?" Wesley said. "Look, Sage, I get where you're coming from. But I'm worried about how close you are to the case. I'm worried it's gonna cloud your judgement, make you see something that... isn't there."

Taylor's eyes flared against his. "What are you saying, Wesley?"

He took a breath. "You think this is the same guy, don't you? You think this is the guy who took your sister."

Wesley just laid the cards out on the table.

Taylor swallowed hard, her jaw tightening. She didn't say anything, but Wesley knew the truth when he saw it; she really did think it was the same guy who'd snatched her sister.

Wesley tried to keep his tone even, but he knew that every word he said was a risk, and could change her mind.

"I know it is," she said.

Wesley felt his chest tighten. He didn't want her to say that. They'd been partners for barely a month. He didn't want to be at odds with her. But her response was making him think whatever they found here wouldn't be good.

"Sage, please," he said. "What we need most is your objectivity. And I'm worried that you don't have it."

"You don't believe me," she said.

Wesley shook his head. "I didn't say that. I'm just saying... I'm worried about you." He stepped toward her. They were so close now, he could feel the heat from her body. "What do you want from me, Sage?" he said, lowering his voice.

Wesley could see the turmoil in her eyes: the longing for answers, for closure. But he also saw her fear of what she might find out.

"Your sister went missing two decades ago," Wesley reasoned. "It's too distant to be related."

"We don't know that." Taylor's expression morphed into a sneer. "You don't have to play devil's advocate with me, Wesley. I know it might not be the truth. But it's worth looking into. I'm not crazy."

Wesley sighed. That was the problem with having a partner. You always had to be in lockstep with them. They couldn't have conflicting feelings or opinions. They had to be one mind.

He took a step back.

"Look, I'm sorry," Wesley said. "I don't want to fight with you. We just have to be on the same page, or this case is going to make one of us crazy."

Taylor sighed, then turned away from him. "I know."

He reached out a hand toward her, but she stepped away.

"Sage..." he said, but she cut him off.

"Can we please get going? I had another idea of where we should look."

Wesley sighed, but nodded. They started walking down the sidewalk. He couldn't deny that he sensed something off on this island, considering there were girls going missing.

"So what's this new idea?" he asked.

"I was thinking—the first girl ran away six months ago, and we've now had three 'runaways' since." Taylor's eyes met his. "I was thinking we should talk to some locals and see if anyone new has moved to the island."

Maybe they moved from Baltimore, Taylor told herself. *Maybe they were near where Angie disappeared, and now they're here...*

Wesley nodded. "Yeah, that makes sense."

They reached the boardwalk, where they emerged into the main part of town. The boardwalk was lined with vendors and stores. The scent of wet fish hung in the air, and the sound of seagulls crying drowned out any other noise around them.

They walked down the boardwalk, and it was bustling. The streets were lined with shops and restaurants and people. In the summer, it was a hotbed of activity, but today there were still a lot of people. They walked by tables of people selling pies and fried dough, giving away candy as they passed, flapping their arms and yelling.

Wesley didn't know who they should talk to first, but he let Taylor take the lead. They approached an older couple who were sitting on a bench watching the ocean.

"Excuse me," Taylor said. "I was wondering if you could answer a few questions for me."

The couple looked up at her, and they were smiling.

"Sure, honey," the wife said. "What's on your mind?"

"I'm with the FBI, and I'm investigating the recent disappearance of four teenage girls."

“Four?” the wife gasped. “I heard about the one girl, but what about the others?”

“By recent, I mean in the past year,” Taylor said. “You may not have heard about the other girls.”

"And was there something in particular you wanted to ask?" the husband asked.

"Yeah, I was wondering if you could tell me... are there any new people that have moved in the area?"

The couple exchanged a look.

"Well, there's a new family that moved to the island," the wife said.

"In the last, say, six months?" Taylor asked.

"Little more than eight, I'd say."

"Are they friendly?" Wesley asked, trying to keep his tone casual.

The wife shrugged. "They're friendly enough. It's just a single dad, Randy, and his children. He lets his kids run free, and they don't abide by our neighborhood rules. They make trouble, but they always say they're sorry after."

"What kind of trouble?" Taylor asked. Wesley could see she was getting way too into this.

"I don't know. I just heard some yelling coming from their house the other night, but they always keep the blinds drawn."

"So they wouldn't let you into the house," Taylor said.

The wife nodded.

"How many kids do they have?" Wesley asked.

The couple exchanged a look.

"I think three," the husband said. "But only the two youngest are troublemakers. They're twins, only eight, I think. But he has an older daughter too. She has to be at least eighteen."

"And how do you know this?" Wesley asked.

"She's very pretty. She goes to the high school. I saw her working in the store a couple months back."

"And what does she look like?" Taylor asked.

The wife thought on it. "Well, she has long, dark hair, and very light eyes."

That detail stuck out—even to Wesley.

So far, every missing girl had those features.

Wesley and Taylor exchanged a look—one that told them it might be a good idea to visit the father of this girl.

CHAPTER THIRTEEN

Taylor's stomach curled with anticipation. As she and Wesley walked down the suburban street, they made out the house that Randy—the new guy in town—apparently lived at. The street was lined with two-story houses, mostly made of paneling, each with its own driveway, porch, and brick path leading to the front door. Roses grew in even rows across the top of the tall white picket fence that surrounded Randy's house.

There wasn't much to go on, based on what the old couple had said, other than that the guy was new to town. But the fact that he had a teenage daughter, one who vaguely matched the resemblance of the missing girls, had definitely given Taylor pause. It felt significant somehow—but she had no idea why.

Either way, she intended to find out.

They approached the house. A man in his forties was spraying down a car, the water glistening in the late day sun. A young girl was with him. This must have been his daughter. They were laughing and having fun, by the looks of it.

The man's voice was loud and booming, the kind of voice that brought people to attention. It was deep, but not unpleasant. He shouted something at his daughter, who giggled and shouted something back as she flopped a giant sponge on the hood of the car.

It was a heart-warming sight. Father and daughter bonding. Not exactly the look of a vicious kidnapper, and Taylor felt a tinge of guilt for being suspicious of such a flimsy statement. This was starting to feel like a wild goose chase, but she pushed on.

When Taylor and Wesley approached them, the father and daughter both stopped fooling around and looked over.

"Evening," Wesley said.

Randy's eyes snapped to them. He set down his hose, then turned off the nozzle. "Hi, folks. How can I help you?"

He was tall, fit, with dark hair that was peppered with gray. He wore an old-fashioned cap, and his face was tanned. From working outside, no doubt. He looked like a friendly guy. He had little beads of water on his forearm, and he wiped them off with the back of his hand.

"Are you Randy?" Taylor asked, stepping closer to him, her jaw squared and her face stern—just in case he was, somehow, their guy.

"I am," he answered. "Who are you?"

"We're with the FBI," Wesley said, stepping forward too.

"We're looking into the disappearance of Amy Schuler," Taylor added.

The man's daughter had recognition flicker across her face.

"Oh, I heard about that!" Randy said. "I really hope they find her soon. I'd be worried sick if my Katelyn went missing."

Katelyn looked down at her feet. She bit down on her lip, likely a nervous habit, showing off her gap tooth.

"Do you know her, Katelyn?" Taylor asked her.

The girl stiffened, her eyes growing large.

"Not super well, but… she was in my class," she said. She walked forward, standing beside her father, who didn't show any signs of being nervous at all. Taylor was beginning to seriously doubt his guilt. "Is she alright?" Katelyn asked. "I heard people are saying she ran off or something?"

"We're not sure," Wesley said.

"Did Amy ever mention she'd be leaving town?" Taylor asked.

The girl shook her head. She immediately went back to playing with the sponge, but she was shaking. Taylor eyed her—it seemed like she had something to add, but was afraid of the consequence.

"If you know anything," Taylor said, "you need to share it with us."

"I don't!" Katelyn exclaimed. "But when I heard people were saying she ran away, I totally didn't buy that."

Taylor felt vindicated by her words. One of Amy's own classmates didn't buy the story that was being pushed. But she needed to know more.

"What makes you say that?" Taylor asked.

Katelyn didn't say anything for a second, instead she glanced at her father.

"It's okay, Katie," he said.

"I just know that Amy loved her life here," she mumbled. "There's no way she ran off."

"What if she was being bullied?" Taylor asked. "Is that a possibility?"

Katelyn sighed. She kept playing with the sponge, which soaked up the water and turned a dark purple. "If there was bullying," she said, "I would totally know about it. Amy—she would come to me if something was wrong. We were friends like that. She told me all about everything in her life, like who she had a crush on and all that."

Taylor nodded, now more convinced than ever that this was a kidnapping. She glanced over at Randy, who offered a smile. Taylor had no reason to suspect him. Nothing at all. And while Katelyn did look somewhat similar to the other missing girls, it just wasn't enough to suspect Randy. Why would he kidnap women who look like his daughter? It made no sense.

This was a dead end. Randy was just a normal dad, and Taylor was, once again, looking for things where they didn't exist. She felt ashamed and exhausted. A whole day's work had led her nowhere.

Taylor nodded at the family. "Thank you for your time."

With that, she and Wesley walked away, down the sidewalk.

It was almost five o'clock, and the sun was dipping toward the horizon, the sky growing dimmer. Taylor's feet were hot and sweaty, even in her sneakers. Her t-shirt was wet, her skin flushed from the heat. She could feel the sweat trickling down the inside of her thighs. But as the sun sank, a cooler wind blew in.

"You don't suspect them, do you?" Wesley asked. Their shoes scraped against the sidewalk as they walked down the quiet suburb.

"No," Taylor said.

Wesley seemed oddly relieved by this. "You seem sure," he said.

Taylor shrugged. "The guy was too friendly, and his daughter seemed normal. She was sad about Amy, but she didn't seem to know anything. I have nothing to suspect either of them over."

"You don't think she was lying?"

Taylor shook her head. "No. I think she was telling the truth."

Wesley nodded. "Yeah, me too."

They rounded the corner, heading toward an intersection. There were people milling about, mowing their lawns, and children playing hopscotch. It was a peaceful island. Taylor imagined raising a family here would be extremely comforting—if not for the disappearances. There was surprisingly more crime here than she would expect from a place like this, but then again, looks could be deceiving; Taylor knew that all too well.

"So we're back where we started," Wesley said. "We have no leads. No idea where to go next. I don't even know if we should keep investigating this case. At least not until we run it by the chief."

Taylor inclined her head to the side. She didn't know what to say to that. Being an agent was all well and good, but they'd been stumbling in the dark all day.

What was the point of continuing? What if they tried, and they failed? That would mean that three girls would remain missing. And that they, Taylor and Wesley, were the failure. That they couldn't get the job done.

She wouldn't be able to live with herself if she quit now. If Amy was never seen again, or if more girls went missing, then Taylor would always blame herself for not doing more. She couldn't just give up. Not yet. And for now, it was best to keep this off the books—not because Taylor didn't think it was a legitimate case, but she was worried that Winchester might somehow see her personal connection and tell her she was too close to work it. And maybe she was; but as far as Taylor was concerned, this was her case.

A bird burst from a tree, landing on a low branch. Up ahead, a pickup truck was driving by, and something about it was familiar. So familiar that it shocked her. Taylor's breath caught in her throat. She stopped dead in her tracks.

Taylor looked at the man who was passing by, although he didn't see her. He was older, maybe fifty or sixty, but he had features that she recognized. He had a shock of gray hair, and he was dressed in blue jeans, a white t-shirt, and a cowboy hat. His face was wrinkled, but Taylor knew she had seen him before.

But where? She wracked her brain for the memory, until like a wave, it hit her.

She had known him when she was young.

The vehicle, an old pickup truck, looked to be well past its prime, from the rust on the body, to the dusty body of the vehicle. The old, weathered, blue paint stood in sharp contrast to all other colors in the area. The bed, though obviously not in good shape, was painted white. The smell of cigarette smoke and motor oil followed the truck.

"Sage?" Wesley cut in, breaking Taylor's reverie.

But she ignored him. Instead, she ran at the truck and tried to flag it down, waving her arms.

She knew him. And every fiber of her being was telling her that they needed to talk—now.

But the truck kept driving. Taylor could barely contain herself. She sprinted after the vehicle, sprinted down the sidewalk, sprinted as fast as she could. Her feet pounded painfully against the road, but the truck was already too far away, and it was turning off into a subdivision, onto a quiet street.

"What the hell are you doing?" Wesley asked. He tried to grab her, but she shrugged him off as she stopped running.

It was too late. He was gone.

But Taylor's mind was reeling. She knew that man's face from before—she never forgot a face. It was an ancient memory, deep within her childhood... but one thing she was certain of was that she didn't know him from Brock Island.

She knew him from Baltimore.

She tried to dive into her memory, to remember who he was. Then, it hit her.

Taylor remembered that when she was seven or eight, her family had adopted a cat for a little while, despite her dad's allergies. They'd found it hurt on the side of the road and had decided to take it in. Taylor's dad wasn't happy, and his eyes were all puffy and red for weeks until he finally adjusted to the cat. It was the only pet the family ever had.

One time, the cat got outside and got in a fight with another cat, and it ended up scratched up pretty bad. So, they brought it to the vet.

Taylor remembered walking into the office, the sterile whites, the smell of dog food and fur in the damp air. Her mother had taken Taylor and Angie to the appointment. She was extremely distressed about the cat and wanted it to get better more than anything.

They went into the office, and there he was—the same man she'd just seen now.

She and her mom talked to him for a few minutes, before the appointment. He had struck Taylor as an odd guy for a vet. He stunk of cigarettes and was gruff, with a long white ponytail, and he droned on too much about politics. She also remembered that he offered Angie a treat to feed to the cat, and Angie had ecstatically taken it. She'd always loved animals. But then later on, Taylor distinctly remembered Angie telling her that the vet "gave her the creeps" and was "looking at her funny."

His name was...

"Smith," she said. "Dr. Smith."

"What?" Wesley asked, raising an eyebrow like Taylor had totally lost her mind.

"That man," she said, pointing toward the direction in which he'd driven. "I know who he is."

It couldn't be a coincidence. What were the chances? The man had known Angie in the same community she'd disappeared from. And now, all these years later, here he was in another community, where girls who looked like Angie were going missing.

No, this was no accident.

CHAPTER FOURTEEN

Taylor could tell Wesley didn't believe her by the look on his face. She could see the doubt, the skepticism, and the guilt in his eyes. He was as skeptical as a man could be, but inside he was upset. Maybe he'd changed his mind; maybe he didn't want to be there with her anymore.

But Taylor had brought him into this, and she hoped he'd stick by her side. This "coincidence" was huge, too huge to ignore. *Just trust me, Wes...*

"His last name's Smith," she said. "He used to have a vet clinic in Baltimore."

"You just seem really sure of this," Wesley said, clearly not buying it.

"I am," Taylor said, and she began pacing up the sidewalk.

"What are you doing?" Wesley asked her, jogging slightly after.

"I need to find that man," she said. "We need a list of everyone on the island with the last name Smith. Then we can narrow down where he lives."

"No," Wesley said. "That's a bad idea. You're too emotionally invested in this, Sage. How do you know his last name is even Smith? Maybe you're mistaking him for someone else. We could be wasting more time."

Taylor faced him. "Why are you fighting me on this?"

"I just don't see how it's connected to Amy Schuler's disappearance," Wesley said.

"Because my sister went missing two decades ago, and that guy—he knew her. And now, all this time later, other girls are going missing, and here he is again. You think that's a coincidence, Wesley? You're an agent. You think about it."

Wesley hesitated. His expression was drawn. Clearly, he was puzzling it out, but Taylor knew he just didn't believe her. Convincing him was a waste of time; Taylor didn't invite Wesley here to be her babysitter, she invited him to be her partner. She didn't care what Wesley thought about her at the moment. She had to do something.

"Listen," she said, putting her hands on her hips. "I understand if you don't believe me. But I'm telling you, I have to do this. Probably not just for Amy, but for my sister, too. I have to know what's happening here. Why is he on the island, and why is he involved?"

Wesley considered this. "Okay," he said. "We can do this. But slowly. And don't get too trigger happy. If you haven't seen the guy in over two decades, you could be mistaking him for someone else. I just want you to acknowledge that possibility."

"It's him," Taylor said. "I know it is. Let's go talk to the sheriff and get those names."

***

The sky was already darkening by the time Taylor reached the Brock Island police station with Wesley. The sun was setting early, and Taylor wondered if a storm was going to hit them soon, judging by the sudden swollen feeling in the air. She hoped not—the last thing she needed was more rain on her parade.

They walked into Sheriff Garth's office, and he didn't look happy to see them. The walls of Garth's office were lined with newspapers and police reports and other documents that had become yellowed and brittle over the years. Sheriff's badges were hung above the desk like ghostly badges of honor, and an empty picture of what must have once been a handsome man was tacked up to the wall. The sheriff's deputy was slumped in the corner, head bowed over a computer screen, and he didn't even look up as they entered.

Garth's face was stern and his eyes looked tired. The air in the small room was musty, like it hadn't been aired out in a long time, like it had just held its breath.

"Great, you two are back again," he said.

"We just need a minute of your time," Taylor explained. "I need to know how many people live on this island with the last name Smith."

Garth laughed, leaned back in his chair. "You think I know that off the top of my head?"

Taylor lifted a brow, waiting for him to fess up and stop messing around. This was a small community. She was willing to bet a year's salary that Garth knew every single person by name.

Garth sighed, letting his demeanor fall off. "There are three people here with the last name Smith."

"Did any of them used to be a veterinarian in Baltimore?" Taylor asked, hope in her chest.

"I sure as heck don't know that," Garth said.

Of course he wouldn't, but it was worth a shot. "Well, can you tell me about each Smith?" Taylor asked.

"Smith's your most common last name in the United States," Garth said. "Can't expect me to keep track of all of 'em."

If that were the case, then Taylor would just have to do the dirty work of investigating them herself.

"I'm going to need their addresses, Sheriff Garth."

"I don't give out addresses," Sheriff Garth said.

"Then I'll find them on my own," Taylor explained. "But this is an FBI investigation now, so your cooperation would be truly appreciated."

Taylor kept her voice clipped, her demeanor professional, despite the fact she sort of wanted to kick Garth in the shin.

"Look, I just don't like you," Garth said. "And I don't like your friend over there. I've been here a long time, and I don't need two kids coming in here and interrupting my work."

"You don't have to like us," Taylor said. "Just give me the addresses."

Garth shook his head. "I'd rather just forget about this."

Wesley stepped forward, opening the file he'd been given. "Sir," he said, "I think you should hear us out. Special Agent Sage has a good reason to believe that one of the Smiths could be connected to this case. We just want a word with them."

Taylor shot Wesley a thankful smile. Garth was clearly old school and didn't respect Taylor enough to hand over the info. It pissed her off that he'd give it to Wesley instead, but whatever got results was fine.

Garth grunted, and he seemed to consider Wesley's words. "I'll listen to you," he said, "because you've got the look of a young man who wants to make something of himself."

Sexist asshole, Taylor thought.

Garth took out a notepad and a pen. "Here's the Smiths' addresses."

Taylor's heart was beating fast. She glanced at the addresses, and she wasn't sure what she was going to find, but she had a feeling that one of these Smiths was not just a local on the island. He was up to something, something dangerous.

Something that could go back as far as Angie's disappearance.

"Good luck," Garth said. "I hope you find what you're looking for."

Taylor and Wesley left the station and began walking down the road, headed toward the first Smith house. A guy named Peter. The evening air was brisk, but they still had at least an hour of daylight left.

"Sage," Wesley said.

Taylor didn't like that tone—it was apprehensive. Again.

They stopped and faced each other on the sidewalk, under the dimming sky. Wesley's black hair was spiked from the sweaty day walking around. Taylor already knew what he was thinking—that this was too personal, and that she was going in too deep.

"Wesley, I'm not gonna pressure you to keep doing this with me," she said. "You can stay, or you can go. It's up to you. But I have to keep doing this."

Wesley studied her face. Taylor felt like he could see through her like a book.

She wasn't in her professional mind. If only he knew the half of it.

"I told you I'd be with you every step of the way," Wesley said. "We're in this together. You said we're a team, right?"

"But you're worried," Taylor said.

Wesley frowned, but nodded. "Yeah. I'm worried about you. You're too invested."

"I can't just sit back and do nothing," Taylor said. "I need answers."

"I know, Sage, just..." He sighed. "Be careful.

Taylor looked at Wesley and smiled. He was coming from a good place; she knew that. But then the feeling passed, and she was back in the air, being dragged down by worry.

"Come on," she said, and headed toward the long, empty road. "Let's go find out what Peter Smith is all about."

Taylor and Wesley walked toward Peter Smith's house. The wind began to kick up, causing the trees to rustle and flutter. The afternoon had been sunny and warm and clear, but now the sky was turning overcast, and it didn't look like this was going to pass quickly. Taylor figured they only had half an hour before the storm hit.

Many of the houses on Brock Island were small, single-story homes. Each one was painted a bright color, like they were trying to cheer themselves up in an out of the way place. Most of them had lights on inside, and Taylor wondered who was home. She wondered if she'd ever crossed paths with any of the residents here back when she was a child.

The world back then was simpler. She had Angie. She had a family. Now, it was like there was lead in her stomach, twisting and knotting and pulling her down.

Taylor found herself wondering what Angie looked like now . . . if her hair was still long and black, if her skin was still pale, if she still laughed at the wrong time during movies.

Maybe this whole thing had been some unhinged, crazy pursuit. Maybe Wesley was right. But Taylor had to remind herself what she was doing this for.

It was for Angie. And every other girl like her. For Amy, and all the others who went "missing" and it was passed off like they were runaways.

When they finally neared Peter Smith's house, Taylor saw it was a cottage-like home on a tiny property. It was painted a pale green and had that sort of outward appearance that indicated a little whimsy. But it was clean and tidy. The windows were clear and the paint was fresh. There were flowers on the porch. A small tin wind chime hung between the front doors. It wasn't fancy, just homey. The smell of cut grass and wildflowers filled the air as they approached.

But the pickup truck was nowhere in sight. *Damn it—this might not be our guy.*

Either way, they were here, and Taylor intended on knocking.

Taylor and Wesley stepped up onto the porch, and Taylor knocked on the door. She was nervous. Their whole plan was to simply knock on the door and see what there was to see. After a few moments, the door opened. An elderly man, possibly as old as ninety, answered the door with a grandfatherly smile.

Taylor's stomach bottomed out. There's no way this was the right Smith.

"Can I help you?" the man asked.

"Are you Peter Smith?" Taylor asked.

"That's me." Peter Smith was aging, and had a few wrinkles and white hair, but he was spry. He was wearing a brown cardigan sweater and some gray dress pants. He was a grandfatherly man, the kind you'd expect to see in a Norman Rockwell painting. The old man seemed kind and genuine.

Taylor didn't know what to say. She glanced at Wesley, but he was equally stumped.

"I'm sorry," Taylor said. "We've got the wrong house."

She and Wesley turned to leave. The man watched them as they walked down the steps. "Are you sure?" he yelled after them. "I could always use some new neighbors!"

Taylor smiled and waved over her shoulder. "I'm sorry to have bothered you, sir."

Peter Smith waved as Taylor and Wesley walked off. Once out of his sight, Taylor let out a frustrated grunt.

"Sorry, Sage," Wesley said.

"It's fine, just more wasted time," Taylor said, looking up at the dark and cloudy sky. "And we're running out of it."

Wesley picked up his pace. "Then I guess we'd better get to Smith Number Two's house."

CHAPTER FIFTEEN

Wesley wanted to have faith in his partner, but this whole thing was getting too weird. As they walked toward the last Smith house, Taylor stormed ahead like Wesley had never seen her—her steps thundered louder than the growing storm in the dark sky above their heads.

The second house had been another dead end—it belonged to a woman with the last name Smith, and that simply didn't fit the profile. That was when Taylor had started to become more agitated.

"This last one has gotta be him," she ranted. Even Wesley, with his long stride, was struggling to keep up with her pace.

"I believe you, Sage, but slow down a second."

"No, Wes, we need to do this now."

It was like there was a fire in her. Taylor was ready to hit something. And there was nothing Wesley could say or do to stop her. She was fuming. She was out for blood.

They had just passed the last house on the road, so Taylor and Wesley were walking around the island, headed toward the next neighborhood. Wesley noticed that Taylor's fingers were twitching at her sides like a time bomb.

She was going to find this Smith guy and then she was going to get her answers—Wesley could tell not even a hurricane would stand in her way. At this point, Wesley was starting to think his new job was to keep her out of trouble. She was losing her grip. He could tell. And he didn't know how to handle it; he had all the respect for Taylor as an agent, but damn, this woman was in too deep. What worried him more than anything was what could happen if this Smith lead didn't lead her to answers about her sister.

Taylor was hoping too much. And Wesley knew how dangerous hope could be in the wrong hands.

Taylor's sister had gone missing two decades ago. Statistically, it was just... impossible for her to be alive. Would Taylor be able to stomach it when that time came? Or would she shatter into a million pieces? He knew she was strong; he didn't doubt that. But even the strongest people had weak spots, and Wesley could see that Taylor's sister was hers.

Thunder cracked and rumbled as the storm gathered strength. The wind was picking up, and so was the water. Wesley could hear the waves viciously slapping against the shoreline. He imagined the white caps were coming in, the waves getting higher and higher.

The trees were thinning on the street. They were close to Garrett Smith's house now, and it was getting darker by the minute. Wesley felt like the darkness was closing in on them, like it was ready to swallow them whole.

A quarter-mile down the road, the houses grew larger, but still stood single-story, painted in bright colors, lights glowing from behind curtains and open upstairs windows. The rain picked up, soaking Wesley's shirt.

When they got to Garrett Smith's house, it wasn't hard to tell which one it was. The front gate was covered in vines, which dripped with yellow leaves that sagged down like leaves on a dying tree. The dirt around the fence was overgrown with weeds, and the white brick of the house had faded to a dirty gray.

And in the driveway was the pickup truck.

Wesley watched as Taylor registered this. Paused for a moment. Then, she approached the house. The front lawn was overgrown with grass and weeds, and the front door and windows needed a fresh coat of paint. The porch light was broken, and the screen door was covered with huge patches of brown rust.

A crack of thunder bellowed, followed by a flash of lightning. Damn. They needed to get shelter, and something told Wesley the interaction at this guy's house was not going to be friendly.

Taylor and Wesley walked up the steps to the front door. Taylor lifted her hand, about to knock, when the door swung open.

She took a step back, and she felt Wesley move beside her.

"What do you think you're doing?"

Garrett Smith was in the doorway. He was standing, but he looked like he had the flu. His eyes were bloodshot and his skin was pale, almost gray. He was thin and there was a dark, sunken ring around each of his eyes. He was wearing a tattered bathrobe and slippers, and his near-white hair was long, flowing around his shoulders.

The man was only standing up because of the cane he was leaning on with his right hand. He looked like a skeleton. Wesley still wasn’t totally convinced Taylor really knew who this guy was.

"I said, what are you doing here?" he demanded, looking like he was struggling to keep his eyes open.

"Dr. Smith?" Taylor said, her voice trembling.

"Doctor?" He lifted an eyebrow. "Just who the hell are you?"

Wesley had a bad feeling in his gut. "We're with the FBI," he quickly said. "We're looking into the disappearance of Amy Schuler. I'm sure you've heard of it."

"I have," Garrett said, still eyeing Taylor, who glared back at him.

"Do you mind if we come in and have a word?" Taylor asked through gritted teeth.

Wesley was getting nervous now. If he didn't know any better, he'd think Taylor was about to snap on this guy. Which wouldn't be like her, but everything about today had been odd. Wesley understood, in many ways; most people lose their sanity when it comes to family. And Taylor's family had been torn apart for twenty years.

Wesley had to admit, if this guy really was a vet Taylor knew as a kid, that was a hell of a coincidence. It was certainly worth looking into, and he didn't think Taylor was "crazy" by any means. He was just worried about her.

Garrett Smith hesitated to let them in. More thunder and rain came down and pounded against the awning of his porch.

"Well, it is storming," Garrett said. "You two better come in, at least until it passes."

"Thank you," Taylor said, her voice just above a whisper.

Fucking hell.

Wesley knew that tone in Taylor's voice, and it wasn't good.

She seemed like a different person now. She was still angry, but her determination had morphed into something else. She was calm, but Wesley knew that calm was just the eye of the storm. He could feel it. He had sensed it earlier—she was on the edge of exploding.

Wesley's anxiety grew as the three of them got into the house. Garrett Smith was limping, which didn't help Wesley's paranoia. They all walked down a long hallway, lined with framed photos. Lightning flashed, followed by thunder, then it was dark again. Taylor's eyes scanned the photos as she walked down the hallway. Wesley could tell she was looking for something, but he didn't know what. Maybe her sister?

Garrett led them into the dark living room. It was messy, like someone had started to clean, then quickly abandoned it. There were stacks of papers everywhere. Unwashed dishes in the kitchen sink, which could be seen through the doorway. And in the middle of the floor was a cardboard box filled with more papers.

Garrett's pictures were hung on the wall, along with a few pictures of family. A beautiful little girl, with her mother. There were pictures of them on the beach, and in the park.

Garrett picked up an empty bottle of tequila from the floor and set it down on the coffee table. The house smelled of stale sweat mixed with stale beer. Garrett himself smelled like he hadn't had a bath in a while.

"I didn't know I'd be having guests," Garrett said. "Have a seat." He motioned to the couch.

Wesley and Taylor sat down. There was a pile of unopened mail sitting on the coffee table, and Garrett moved it to the floor.

"You said you worked for the FBI," Garrett said, his voice deep and low.

"Yes," Taylor said. Sitting on the couch next to Wesley, her body was jittering. He kept an eye on her in his periphery. "I'm sure you heard about the missing teenage girl, Amy Schuler."

"I did, yeah. How can I help?"

"How long have you lived on Brock Island, Mr. Smith?" Taylor asked, her voice tense.

Garrett warily eyed both agents. At this point, maybe he was realizing he was a suspect. "About two years now."

"Like it much?" Taylor asked. There was a fury in her eyes that put Wesley on edge.

"It's all right," Garrett said.

"And where did you live before?"

At that point, Garrett was looking extremely apprehensive. Garrett's breath hit the air in a cloud of alcohol and stale smoke. More thunder growled outside.

He wasn't answering the question.

"I thought you said you were looking into the Schuler girl's disappearance? Why are you asking about my life?"

"Just trying to get to know you," Taylor said, her voice low and deadly. "And all of the residents here on the island."

"Uh huh," Garrett said, almost like he wasn't buying it. "Well, if you're with the FBI, I guess I don't have anything to worry about."

Taylor stared at Garrett, who was looking down at his hands. His knuckles were white as he gripped his cane.

"You know, we haven't formally introduced ourselves," Wesley said, trying to defuse the tension. They were getting nowhere this way. "My name is Wesley, and I'm a special agent with the FBI."

"Nice to meet you," Garrett said, barely glancing up. He was playing with his cane, but not like he was nervous. More like he was resting it on his knees, tapping it against his legs.

"And I'm his partner," Taylor said. "Special Agent Taylor Sage."

There was a flicker of recognition on Garrett's face. But he just said, "Well, I'm happy to help any way I can. You got any questions about Amy or are we just here to talk about me?"

"We're trying to get to know everyone in town," Taylor explained coolly. "Where did you live before you moved to Brock Island, Mr. Smith?"

"Baltimore," he answered without hesitation.

Shit, Wesley thought. This really was the same guy. His heart rate began to pick up. What if Sage was right?

"Lived there my whole life," Garrett explained. "Great place, but I'd always dreamed of island life, and when my wife left me, I realized I had nothing left there so I retired and came here."

"It sounds nice," Wesley said, trying to ease the tension in the air.

"It's all right," Garrett said, shaking his head. "Not what I expected, but that's life, right?" At that, he smiled again. It was a strained, crooked smile, but it was something.

"You said your wife left you," Taylor said, her voice still low and ominous.

"She went back to her high school ex," Garrett said, practically spitting the words out. "She'd left him earlier, but she came back when I retired. Had a change of heart, I guess. And a few weeks later she left with him."

"Tough luck," Wesley said.

"I guess we don't always get what we want," Taylor added.

"You could say that," Garrett said, laughing. He coughed and shook his head, then waved a hand. Then, his eyes fixed on Taylor. "You know... something about you is familiar."

The air in the room stood still. The tension rose up, thick and oozing.

"Is that so?" Taylor said. "I admit, I'm not surprised, considering you knew me and my family."

Garrett's eyes flashed. "The hell are you talking about?"

"Does the name Angie Sage mean anything to you?"

Now it was getting real. Wesley braced himself. All at once, Garrett seemed to remember.

"The Sage family!" he exclaimed. "You used to bring your kitten to my vet clinic in Baltimore. What a small world."

Taylor was trembling. Wesley kept eyeing her, wondering what her next move would be. But she stayed quiet and let Garrett finish.

"I did hear about what happened to your sister," he said. "I remember it well, even joined in on the search party, but... they never found Angie, the poor girl."

Taylor shot up to her feet. "Don't you say her name."

Garrett was flabbergasted. "What?"

Wesley stood too, hoping to keep the situation under control—but it was too late.

Taylor stormed up to Garrett.

CHAPTER SIXTEEN

Taylor could feel her heart pulsing, threatening to break free from her chest. The adrenaline was strong and tasted acidic in her mouth.

All sensibilities had left her.

She got right in Garrett Smith's face and looked deep into his eyes. This was him. This was the man who took Angie and who took Amy Schuler and all those other girls—he had to be.

If he wasn't, then Taylor didn't know what she would do.

All Taylor could see was red. She could feel the blood pumping through her veins. It was like the animal part of her brain had taken over, and she was just another beast unleashed from its cage. She never raised a hand—that wasn't her style, but she wanted him to know that she knew the truth.

"You," she said. "You did this."

"Sage," Wesley said, but she could barely hear him above the sound of her own heart.

"You're the one who took Angie," Taylor said. She was backing him into a wall. "You took my sister."

"Whoa, whoa, whoa," Garrett said, his face white. "I didn't have anything to do with that! I only met the girl one time!"

"Where the hell are they, Smith?" Taylor demanded. "Where's Angie? Where's Amy Schuler?"

"I don't know, I swear, I don't know what you're talking about," Garrett said. He was freaking out, and he looked almost like he was about to cry. "I didn't have anything to do with any of that."

"It seems that young girls go missing wherever you are, Mr. Smith."

"Really, I swear, I have no idea what you're talking about," Garrett said. He looked down, away from her. "If I knew anything, I'd help you out, I swear."

Taylor trembled. "No. You're lying."

"Sage, step back." Wesley grabbed her shoulder. His warm hand seemed to bring her back to reality, because as soon as he touched her, Taylor realized she was being way more aggressive than she ever had been before. She would feel ashamed, but her blood was still pumping so hard. Either way, she backed off and Garrett scrambled away from them. He sat down in the chair, obviously shaken.

"What the hell are you thinking?" Wesley demanded, still holding Taylor.

"That he's lying," Taylor said, seething. "He's lying, and he knows where they are."

"I don't!" Garrett exclaimed. "I swear, I've never taken, hurt, or done anything to any women!"

Taylor went to storm him again, but Wesley grabbed her.

Taylor was still damn convinced Garrett was her guy, but a strong sense of embarrassment and shame surged through her. What the hell was she doing? She'd expect this type of outburst from Wesley, if anything—not from herself. And here he was, holding her, calming her.

Taylor relaxed in his arms, and Wesley let her go. She shook him off and stepped away.

"You need to take five," Wesley said sternly.

Taylor glared at Garrett, then back at Wesley. "I'm not going anywhere. I'm calm now."

Wesley looked doubtful. "Are you sure?" He glanced back at Garrett, then at Taylor. "You're a hell of a lot calmer now than you were a few seconds ago, I'll give you that. Just take five before you go back over there and accuse that guy of kidnapping your sister."

Taylor frowned. Despite her urge to get back to the task at hand, Wesley was right. She was too emotional right now.

"Fine," she said, taking a few steps away to be out of Garrett's earshot.

This time, Wesley followed her. She noticed he was still on edge, but she wasn't sure if it was because of her or Garrett.

"Look, I know you're upset, but you need to get it together," he said. "You can't just go off like that. I'm the unhinged one, remember?" he joked.

"I'm calm now," she insisted, crossing her arms. "I'm fine."

"You sure?" His gaze was hard on hers. "Because if you are, we can go back in there and talk to this asshole. Together. If you're not, we can stay right here until you are."

"I am calm," she said with a nod. "I'm sorry. I know I shouldn't have done that."

"No, you shouldn't have," Wesley said. "I know I'm in no position to lecture anyone about keeping their head on during an emotional case, but this isn't you, Sage. You aren't like this. Maybe I don't know you that well, but I can say that for sure."

Taylor frowned. She deserved that. And she knew she did.

"You're right," she said. "I can admit you're right."

Wesley nodded, and a smile tugged at his lips. "I'm on your side, okay? We'll get answers out of this guy, I promise. Let's get back in there and figure this out."

She nodded, and they walked back to where Garrett was still sitting.

"Can one of you two please explain what's going on here?" he demanded. "As you can see, I'm sitting here, not running, because I'm not guilty of any crime."

Taylor had to admit—the guilty ones usually ran, in her experience, but that didn't make Garrett Smith innocent.

"It is a major coincidence, I've gotta say," Wesley said, crossing his arms over his chest as he stood, towering above Garrett. "You lived in Baltimore near where Special Agent Sage's sister disappeared, and now, all these years later, another girl has gone missing under nearly identical circumstances. You have to admit we have reasonable suspicion here."

"I don't know what to tell ya," Garrett said. "I've lived here for years now, and besides, I may not look like much, but I still have a way with the ladies. Talk to Marge Bennett if you want to know where I've been the last few nights. She's lived here her whole life and she can vouch for me. Didn't that Schuler girl go missing two nights ago?"

An alibi, Taylor thought with dread. But why did she feel dread? She realized that she *wanted* Garrett Smith to be the guy. Because then, all of her questions, her anxieties—they would be solved. Easy as pie. No more wondering. No more anxiety and sleepless nights, no more nightmares about Angie…

But if that wasn't the case, and Garrett was innocent, then that would mean all of this had been in vain, and Taylor was no closer to finding Angie. At that moment, she really wished she was back in Pelican Beach, so she could get a reading from Belasco. Maybe it wouldn't give her answers, but it could give her hope.

"And you're sure you haven't seen these girls?" Wesley said.

"I'm sure," Garrett said. "That's the truth."

Wesley looked at Taylor, his eyebrows raised. It was her call.

She knew, at the end of the day, that there was no proof at the moment.

"I'll tell you what, Smith," Taylor said. "We're gonna leave you alone for a little bit. But I suggest you think about what you've told us. And when we come back, you're gonna tell us everything. And by orders of the FBI, you're prohibited from leaving the island until further notice. Understood?"

Garrett laughed. "Yeah, I'll be at Marge's! You two can see yourselves out, and you're damn lucky I'm not pressing assault charges." He winked at Taylor. "For old time's sake, girly."

She tried not to let him get under her skin. She frowned at him—just something to show that she was the one in control. "I'm sure we'll be seeing each other again soon, then."

"You better believe it," he muttered.

Wesley looked at Taylor. "Let's go."

***

Taylor walked out of the police station with Wesley, grateful the storm had passed, although the nighttime air was still humid. It smelled like a mix of rain, fish, algae, and the salt of the sea.

They'd just spent the last twenty minutes using the police phone to call Marge, Garrett's girlfriend, to confirm his alibi. She claimed they'd gone out for a fancy dinner the night Amy vanished, which was also confirmed by the restaurant. Then Garrett spent the night at Marge's place.

He wasn't the one who took Amy. And so Taylor could only assume he also wasn't the one who took Angie.

Every fear she'd had earlier, about all of this being another goose chase, had come true. Taylor felt defeated. No—she felt useless.

"Well, the alibi checks out," Taylor muttered to Wesley, disappointed.

She felt a warm hand on her shoulder, and looked up to see Wesley giving her a half smile, illuminated by the streetlight behind them. "Don't beat yourself up. We had reasonable cause to believe it was him."

"I know..." Taylor sighed. "It just feels terrible. I feel like a failure. I'm still no closer to finding Amy." *Or Angie.*

That was the worst part of it all. Taylor couldn't bring herself to stop obsessing over the two girls' disappearances. She couldn't stop thinking about what she could have done to have prevented it. And now, she had been so close to catching Garrett—a suspect that she was sure had to be the one who'd taken both girls—and it was snatched away from her.

Taylor was frustrated and angry, and she knew that she would do anything to make it right. But that was the problem—the only way to make it right was to find the real kidnapper. And there wasn't a lead in sight.

"Yeah..." Wesley said, and she could tell he was thinking the same thing.

"And now we've alienated the only potential lead we had on the island," Taylor continued. "If we can't find any other suspects, then it's a dead end."

Wesley stuffed his hands in the pockets of his pants. "It's late anyway, Sage. We should break for the night. Grab a motel, start fresh in the morning."

She nodded. She appreciated the sound advice—but she didn't want to give up. Not yet. However, Taylor was a long way from home, and working off the books. Wesley was right. It was time to call it quits for the night.

They were walking through the quiet streets, away from the police station. The roads were still as empty and quiet as when they left. The wind had calmed, but the chill in her bones sounded like the screeching of dead insects.

Belasco's clues had led Taylor here—but why? She still hadn't found the symbol, but she was certain it once existed here. Plus, Belasco had said someone would "return from her past"—that could have been Garrett Smith, and yet that had led nowhere. Maybe Belasco was wrong about everything; maybe Taylor was too.

The motel was a small building, with a neon sign out front that seemed to be perpetually out of order. It was called the Sun and Moon Inn. Its paint was chipped, its doors hung crooked, and its flower boxes were overgrown. But there was still something quaint and homey about it. Maybe in the various, ocean-themed décor. The place was sort of gaudy, but it seemed clean.

"Let me pop in and grab us some keys," Wesley said.

Taylor nodded and stood outside as Wesley went in, then stared up at the night sky. The storm had passed, and the clouds parted to reveal a half moon. It was hard to believe she had once stood on this very island with her sister. Angie felt so far away that she, herself, had started to feel like the dream. A dream Taylor was senselessly chasing.

She thought of her father, back in the hospital after suffering his heart attack. She had a moment now, so she took out her phone and called her mother. She picked up within a few rings.

"Taylor," her mom said.

"Mom, is Dad okay?"

"He's okay, sweetie. I'm with him at the hospital right now."

"How is he?"

Her mom sighed. "He's still weak, but he's doing better. He's already making demands, asking when he can go home."

"Is he in pain?" Taylor's chest squeezed just thinking about it.

"He's had some painkillers now. He's sleeping. Don't worry about us."

Taylor let out a breath of relief. If she found an answer about Angie, she prayed her father would be able to forgive her, but she still felt terrible for stressing him out.

"I keep thinking back to last night," Taylor said. "I just keep thinking about all the things I could've done differently. The things I should have done differently."

"It hasn't been that long," her mother said. "It's still fresh. Just let it sit with you for a while. It'll come out in the washing. And when you come back home, we can talk more about it. Your father loves you—he'll understand. Just give him time."

She was right, of course, but Taylor still couldn't stop thinking about it. She really was spiraling out of control.

"I will," Taylor said. "I'll call you tomorrow."

"Okay, sweetie. Take care."

Taylor hung up the phone. For a long moment, she stared at the motel in thought. She doubted she'd be getting much sleep tonight.

CHAPTER SEVENTEEN

He sat atop the hill with his binoculars out, watching as so many girls walked along the pier in the early light of day. The pier stretched out into the water, and he looked out over the bay. The sun shone off the water spreading a soft glow into the sky. The air tasted of the sea, and he could already feel a trace of salt on his tongue. It was beautiful.

Through the binoculars, he saw the girls he'd been waiting for all night. They were pretty and cute and everything he'd hoped for in a girl.

But none of them were her.

None of them were his Patricia.

Shutting his eyes, he went back to his youth, to the day he first saw her. She had been so radiant. So beautiful. He was captured immediately.

But Patricia was harsh, too. She was a hurricane. He could still feel the burns on his arm now from when she'd stamp her cigarettes out on his flesh. He remembered the smell of burning hair. The bubbling of his skin.

He had been afraid of her.

But not anymore. Patricia had no power over him. And he could find a new Patricia: a preserved Patricia.

He opened his eyes, and as if it were some sort of cosmic fate, he saw her. A small and skinny brunette with long and flowing hair. Just like his Patricia's.

A sudden jolt of hatred hit his heart. The girl moved delicately along the shoreline. She was on the end of the pier, and even from afar, he could make out the delicate lines of her body. The wind blew her hair out behind her and flowed around her. A loose and flowing striped dress drifted behind her with the light breeze.

Patricia had worn stripes on that day... that day...

That day she hurt him for the first time.

His teeth clenched tight, and he peered through his binoculars to get a closer look. The girl smiled at her friend. Oh, what was that? Her smile looked so much like Patricia's... and her eyes, they matched too.

He had seen this girl on the island before, but never had she stood out to him like in this moment. It was like he was seeing the light for the first time. It must have been the stripes, which reminded him so much of that day all those years ago.

He found himself unable to move his eyes away from the girl. All the other girls in the world disappeared. She was the only one that mattered anymore.

Maybe this girl would be the one. Maybe this girl would be the one he'd been waiting for.

He watched as the girl said something to her friend, then she turned and began to walk away from her. His eyes grew wide with suspicion... or maybe hope.

He decided it, right then and there.

His current catch was not enough.

She was not Patricia.

This new girl, down by the water; she was everything he'd ever dreamed of. She was perfect, and she would love him. Like Patricia did.

But... he only had room for one Patricia in his life.

He stood up and dusted off his shorts.

That meant the other one had to go.

CHAPTER EIGHTEEN

Taylor hated the way the stiff motel mattress felt on her back. But after hours of tossing and turning, feeling so much guilt about her father, Angie, even Garrett Smith—she was finally able to fall asleep.

But it didn't last long before she awoke in a field in her dream.

Angie was there. Her big sister was a little older. She wore a red sweatshirt and jeans—like she had been on the day she disappeared. Only, there was no fear in her eyes, no look of uncertainty. She didn't look like she was going to be taken from Taylor, from their family.

"You're here," Taylor said.

"I'm here," Angie confirmed.

Taylor felt so relieved—almost as if her sister were really there. She had so many questions for her, and so much to say. "I'm so sorry—"

"Don't be sorry," Angie said. "I'm here now." Then she smiled, and her eyes became bright, and bright blue.

Taylor couldn't recall a time when she had ever been so happy and so excited in her life. She had missed her sister so much. And she felt awful that she was the one who had driven her away from home.

She was running towards her with such force that she tripped over the dirt and fell to the ground. Taylor was just so happy to be with her sister, she didn't care.

When she reached her, she embraced her. This was perfect. The moment was perfect. She and her sister were finally together again.

Angie's face was wet with tears, and she was shaking.

But then, suddenly, she wasn't holding anyone at all.

Angie was gone.

When Taylor turned around, they were still in the field, but this time, Angie was far off in the distance.

And there was a man with her.

It was him. The man who took Angie. But he had no face. His head was just a black silhouette, and yet she could feel his glare on her. He held out his hand and Angie took it—and then he pulled her away, and dragged her into the woods.

Panic flooded Taylor's chest. She had to do something. She had to save Angie. But she couldn't. Her feet wouldn't move.

And then Angie was gone again.

Taylor was alone. She was alone now, just as she had been twenty years ago. She had failed again. She had let her sister down.

"I'll never stop looking for you," Taylor said. "I'll find you, Angie. I promise. I promise I'll find you."

Everything around Taylor was white. She was in a strange place—a strange place that was familiar, but not. It was the same place that she had visited when she had "died" after being shot in the abdomen in her twenties, but it was different. She could see the ground beneath her, and the sky above her. She was standing on nothing. She felt like she was going to fall, and when she reached out, she could see her own hand.

She could see her whole body, the way she must look in real life. But she was still standing on nothing.

"Angie?"

Her sister wasn't there.

Taylor felt something then—a presence. Someone was watching her. It was a strange feeling. It wasn't menacing, not really. And yet, she couldn't deny the feeling that she should be afraid.

She turned around.

The feeling was still there, and yet, there was nothing.

She faced forward again.

And this time, she saw something.

It was Angie. It was her, standing on nothing. But it was too far away, like she was seeing herself from a million miles away. She saw everything—the details of her clothing, her hair—but she was still too far away to see her face.

A gust of wind came, and Angie was gone.

With a start, Taylor opened her eyes. The motel room materialized around Taylor. The room echoed as if a large auditorium was empty, and then it was quiet. Her bed was soaked in sweat. She was covered in a sheen of fear.

She looked over at the clock beside her bed—it was 6:37 AM.

Her entire body was shaking, her teeth were rattling. She was so scared that she couldn't even cry anymore.

Then, a knock at the door. Taylor's heart jumped into her throat.

"Sage, it's me," said Wesley on the other side, and Taylor relaxed.

"Hold on!" she said, jumping out of bed. She ran to the door, and pulled it open. He was standing on the other side.

"Morning," Wesley said.

He wore a gray hoodie and jeans. In one hand he had a tray of coffees, the other a brown paper bag. She could smell a hint of bacon through it.

"What are you doing here?" she asked.

"I came to see if you wanted to have breakfast with your partner," he said. "Better to start the day off right."

Hesitantly, Taylor let Wesley in. She was still wearing her sleepwear, but it was just a t-shirt and sweatpants. She always packed light. They sat at the small table by the window, where the early morning sunlight filtered in like gold. Wesley handed her a coffee and a bagel sandwich, and Taylor unpackaged the food. The bacon and egg tasted delicious, and she took a sip of bitter black coffee, feeling slightly more at ease.

Until Wesley said: "Don't kill me, but I talked to Winchester."

Taylor's stomach rolled. She pictured the chief, chewing her out for being careless. "You did?"

"Yeah, he wanted me to come into work, so I had to tell him what I'm up to." Wesley paused. "I tried to keep you out of it so you wouldn't get in shit for working off the clock, since you're supposed to be 'off' right now, Sage, but Winchester could smell you all over this thing. I'm sure you'll get a call from him soon, but I asked him to let us do our work. When he looked into the case himself, he okayed it." He took a bite of his bagel. "So, looks like you and me are officially on the books. The Amy Schuler case is officially our jurisdiction, and the sheriff can't tell us to screw off anymore."

A wash of relief came over her. "Thank you, Wesley."

"Don't thank me," he said. "You're the one who figured out the connection. I'm just here to help you with the grunt work."

Taylor felt a familiar pang of guilt. "I'm the one who screwed up," she said.

"I didn't tell Winchester about your little... episode with Garrett Smith, if that's what you're worried about."

Taylor lifted her brows. "You didn't?"

"Hell no. I've lost my head before too. Remember how aggressive I got with those guys on that last case?"

Taylor nodded with a smile. It was true. Wesley had been high-strung, and aggressive. "It's weird for you to be the level-headed one here," she said with a laugh, hoping to find some humor in this mess she'd gotten them into.

"Very funny," Wesley said dryly, but he was smiling. He took a sip of his coffee.

She sipped her coffee too. "You're not going to get in trouble for this, are you?" she asked.

"Winchester's a good guy," Wesley replied. "He won't throw us under the bus."

"You sure?"

"Yeah," he said. "He knows we're doing good work here."

Wesley's phone suddenly rang, and he took it out. His brows pinched together. "It's my daughter. Gotta take this."

He stood up and walked across the room as he answered, and Taylor focused on finishing her breakfast.

"Hi, sweetie," Wesley said into the phone. Taylor heard a girl's voice on the other end of the line, but she couldn't make out what she was saying. "Yeah, I'm doing well. I'm with a friend right now... no, kiddo, that's not what I mean. I'm working. It's... an investigation. I'm on a case."

Taylor couldn't help but smile as Wesley talked to his daughter. She was finally seeing the warmer side of him—the side of him he'd told her about before. According to Wesley, everything he did in life was for his daughter.

Taylor realized then, as she watched him talk and smile, that it had been a long time since she'd thought about her own infertility. That whole situation somehow felt like another life. Taylor still wanted a family someday. Clearly, it would never be with Ben Chambers. But she knew it would be with someone, someday. She was in no rush to get there. Right now, her mission was to save other people's kids' lives. And she was happy to do it.

Taylor pulled out the files on the missing victims from her case and spread them on the table as Wesley talked to his daughter. There had to be something she wasn't seeing. Some deeper connection between all these girls.

She took out the photo of each girl and spread them on the table.

Amy Schuler. Jessica Clements. Brenda Grimmie. Samantha Skelly.

All eighteen, except for Jessica, who was nineteen.

Angie had been sixteen when she disappeared.

Taylor ignored that discrepancy, focusing on the photos of the girls. Yes, they all had dark hair and light eyes. Pretty. The one who looked most like Angie was Amy, but the others had no real resemblance other than being Caucasian with dark hair and light eyes.

Taylor looked closer at the photographs, at each girl's smile.

Something else struck her, and it made her heartrate pick up. In Amy's photo, she had a tight-lipped smile, not showing teeth. But the other three all had toothy smiles, and it was clear as day: they each had a gap between their teeth.

Maybe it was a coincidence, but Taylor seriously doubted that. To be sure, she took out her phone and looked up Amy Schuler on social media. It didn't take long to find. Amy's profile picture was her with a toothy smile.

And a gap tooth.

Taylor ignored the voice in the back of her head that reminded her that Angie did not have a gap tooth. That didn't matter right now; what mattered was that these four missing girls, while each with different facial features, had striking similarities in every other way.

The gap tooth was a unique detail, something not many people had. Taylor was willing to bet this meant something.

She glanced over at Wesley. He was still talking to his daughter.

Voicing it to him would be the right thing to do, but Taylor had bad feeling he'd shut it down. Before Taylor dug any further, she wanted to get some solid proof that there was a connection. As much as Taylor appreciated Wesley being here and attempting to be a voice of reason, she could also feel his doubts.

For now, she was going to dig into this herself.

She grabbed her phone, flipped it open, and snapped a photo of the line-up of girls. She then took a screenshot of Amy's profile photo and saved it to her phone, and saved the line-up to her photo gallery.

There was something more to this.

CHAPTER NINETEEN

The police station was oddly quiet when Taylor walked up to it with Wesley, the early morning sun hot on the back of her neck. She'd been partially expecting the same crowd of frantic townspeople as yesterday, but maybe they'd all heard the bogus runaway story that the sheriff was pushing.

They entered the police station. The air was stale, musty, the smell of old wood and dust. Sheriff Garth was stapling a photo of Amy Schuler to the bulletin board.

"Garth," Taylor said.

He turned to Taylor and Wesley with contempt. Surely, he knew now that the case had been officially handed to the FBI, and he wasn't happy about it.

The other officers in the station did not look happy either. They were too busy taking care of daily police duties to take much notice of them, but it was clear that they were working on autopilot. The spark had gone out of everyone here.

"Special agents Sage and Wesley," Garth said. "You're late."

Taylor said nothing, just glanced at the missing person's poster. At least now he was taking the case more seriously.

"I wanted to know if you had any information on the families of the other missing girls," Wesley said. "Their current phone numbers. I'd like to talk to them."

"All right," Garth muttered. "Come with me."

He began walking toward his office, and Wesley followed—but Taylor stayed behind.

Wesley turned and gave her a curious look. "You coming?"

Taylor hesitated. "Actually, I was thinking we should split up today. We could cover more ground that way. Since this is now an official case and all. You deal with Garth and the families. I'll… be running down other leads."

Wesley frowned. He walked up close to her so no one else in the office could hear and whispered, "You think that's a good idea? You were a bit out of your head yesterday."

Taylor ignored the flame of embarrassment inside her. He wasn't wrong. She knew she'd acted out of line. But she wouldn't make those mistakes again. "I'm fine," she said.

Wesley didn't look like he believed her.

"Really," she said. "I'm okay. I promise."

"Okay," Wesley said. "But if you start to feel any more... anxious, call me, okay? I'll come bail you out. I'll start contacting the families of the other missing girls and set up a meeting with the sheriff's office to discuss with Winchester." Wesley paused, gray eyes sliding over Taylor. "Stay safe, Sage."

With that, he went and stood outside of Garth's office.

Taylor remained in the main area of the police station. She needed to think of her next move, but she wasn't sure where to begin.

Wesley and Garth returned a minute later. Garth was holding a clipboard of paperwork and handed it to Wesley as they walked. "Here you go. Phone numbers and addresses. Good luck with your investigation."

He handed Wesley the clipboard, then tossed a stack of file folders at him.

"Have a good one, Garth," Wesley said.

Taylor watched in silence as Wesley turned and left the police station. He didn't look back. He was already on to his next task on the case, and Taylor was left alone.

She glanced around the station. The officers were busy with their own work. They were all just trying to keep from going crazy.

Then, a familiar face: Officer Brady. He breezed out of his office, running a hand through his short brown hair, when he spotted Taylor. Taylor walked right up to him. She figured if she could get some more information on local crime over the past while, she might get an idea of where to begin investigating for today.

"Officer Brady," Taylor said.

His eyebrows went up. "Special Agent Sage. You're still here."

"I'm back. I've been officially assigned to this case."

Brady looked like he was about to say something, but then his mouth clicked shut. He gestured for Taylor to follow him. "I've got some time before my shift starts. Let's talk."

Brady led Taylor into his office. The room was tiny and cramped, with a desk, a table and chairs, and a filing cabinet. Taylor sat down across from Brady as he closed the door behind them.

"I'm surprised this is a legitimate FBI case now," Brady said.

"I'm not," Taylor said. "They must know I'm the right person for this."

"I guess so."

She glanced over at the photo on the corner of his desk. Brady was standing next to a young woman with dirty-blonde hair in a high ponytail, a pale face, and bright hazel eyes. Her eyes were staring straight into Taylor's.

"Well, what can I help with?" Brady asked.

"I was wondering if you had any crime reports from the last couple of weeks. Like, before the girls went missing," Taylor said. "I'm looking for anything that strikes me as odd."

He opened the filing cabinet and pulled out a manila folder, flipped through it a few times, and pulled out a photocopied report. "Here's the last report that was submitted. I'll see if I can dig up anything else."

"Thanks," Taylor said as she took the report. "I appreciate it."

She was about to flip open the files when Brady spoke again.

"What do you think happened to the girls?"

Taylor sighed. "I wish I knew."

"You really don't believe the runaway story, huh?"

"Would you if you were in my position?"

"I guess you're right. I think I'd be just as suspicious too," Brady said. "I thought they'd just run off, but I've lived here my whole life. A lot of people do just run away from the island if they hate living here. It can be... isolated."

Taylor thought of everyone in town, how they were all in a tizzy over the girls being gone. She didn't think so. "I don't think these people just ran away."

"But why wouldn't they call home? Or their boyfriends? Someone? That's what I don't get."

"I don't know," Taylor said. "But we're going to figure it out."

With that, Taylor flipped open the file and began skimming the report of recent crimes on Brock Island. Unsurprisingly, most were minor: a few kids getting caught drinking underage, a break-in at a food truck by the beach, some misdemeanors. Nothing major. The report was mostly a litany of juvenile crimes, and Taylor was disappointed. She continued to skim through the pages—and then saw something that made her freeze.

Eight months ago, two women had been assaulted by a man named Alex Hensley. Hensley had been about to sexually assault one of the women when another woman—a stranger—had appeared and scared him off with a gun. Hensley was a landscaper who'd lived on Brock Island for ten years.

Taylor looked up at Officer Brady. "Do you have any more reports of similar crimes as the Hensley case?"

"The Hensley case?" Brady raised his brows. "That happened months ago. That was the only incident involving him. Real weird one, too."

Heart pounding, Taylor read deeper into the report. Her heart sank when she saw that the two women involved in the altercation were twenty-eight and thirty—not close to the age of the girls who had been taken. But that didn't mean they couldn't be related. An assault on the island was a big deal, and maybe Hensley had gone quiet because he'd switched up to kidnapping. Maybe he'd started targeting younger women because the older ones were too much trouble.

Taylor looked up at Brady with fire in her chest. "Does Hensley still live on the island?"

"He sure does," Brady said bitterly. "Was in jail for about a month before he got out on good behavior. None of the women he assaulted were actually injured, just traumatized, so he got off way too easy. He's still on parole, mind you."

It made Taylor sick—too many people got off on crimes like that. Taylor looked at the mugshot of Hensley on the file. He was an older man, at least fifty. His face was gaunt, his body thin, his eyes sunken and dark, his hair was receding. He wore handcuffs and a hospital gown, but he didn't appear intimidated.

"Do you know where he lives?"

"No. But I do know he's always fishing down by the pier."

Taylor was already standing.

"Do you want me to come with you?" Brady asked.

"No," Taylor said. If she had to deal with Hensley by herself, so be it. She didn't trust anyone else but herself to get the job done. She was going to bring him down for the crimes he committed—if he was truly behind the kidnappings on the island.

Taylor clenched her fists. "Which pier does he go to?"

"The southern pier, it's a bit of a walk."

Taylor nodded. "Thanks, Officer Brady. You've been a huge help."

A few minutes later, Taylor was striding out of the police station. She passed by Wesley, who was standing on the pavement and talking on his cell phone. He looked up at her and frowned, but Taylor kept walking. She was on a mission.

The sun was high in the sky, burning down on Taylor and making her skin prickle. The island was hot and muggy, just like yesterday. She ignored the discomfort and started walking, trying to remember the way to the southern pier. She hadn't noticed it the day before, but she wanted to find it now.

It took her ten minutes to find the pier. It connected the mainland to the small beach on the other side of the island. And Taylor was surprised to see it so heavily populated with fishermen. There were probably a hundred men standing on the pier, gaping down into the water in hopes of catching a big one.

She looked around at all the faces, searching for Hensley, but she couldn't see him. She wasn't sure if a man like him would be out so early in the morning—maybe he would be home, sleeping off a night of drinking.

Taylor crept through the crowd of fishermen, trying not to draw attention to herself. She spotted a small supply shack a few dozen feet away from the pier. She walked up to the shack and pushed the door open.

The room was dark and airless, no air conditioning. It was lined with shelves that were stocked with fishing equipment and bait. The room smelled of old fish and saltwater. It smelled of ozone and the swamp and the sea.

There was a man leaning in the corner, his eyes closed. He was holding a fishing pole in his hand, and he was snoring softly. Taylor frowned.

She poked him on his shoulder. "Excuse me, sir?"

The man's eyes shot open. He was a little shorter than Taylor and very stout, with a long nose, his face covered in wrinkles. He was graying at the temples and had a beard. She guessed he was in his mid-sixties.

"Yes?" he asked. "Is something wrong?"

"I need to ask you a few questions," she said. "If you don't mind."

"What?" he asked, his eyes blinking rapidly. "Who are you? What do you want?"

"Taylor Sage," she said. "I'm just visiting the island." She didn't feel like wasting time explaining that this was official police business.

Eyeing Taylor, he stood up from his chair and extended a meaty hand. Taylor reluctantly shook it, surprised by how firm his handshake was.

"Robert Gable," he said. "I own the supply shop here."

Behind the counter was a closed door that must have led to a back room, a fish mount preserved on the wall, and a photo of what looked like Robert when he was young with a woman, but it was too small for Taylor to make out the details. Compared to the rest of the island, which could be touristy, sometimes even rich, the southern side seemed more grassroots.

"I'm looking for a man named Alex Hensley," Taylor said. "Have you seen him today?"

Robert stroked his beard. "Hensley? Yeah, he came in to grab some bait about forty minutes ago. Why, what's this about?"

Taylor ignored his question; she couldn't divulge more. "Do you know where he usually fishes? I need to have a word with him."

"Bright and early. Mornings are the best time to catch the biggest fish." He grinned slightly. "In fact, it's the only time to catch the biggest fish."

Taylor nodded. "Can you show me the spot?"

"He usually fishes right by the end of the pier, so I'm sure you'll find him there."

“Thanks,” Taylor said, and she left. Taylor stepped out of the supply shop into the blazing sun. Her body was hot, and she suddenly felt exhausted.

She looked over the crowd once again, but Hensley was still nowhere to be seen. She saw the end of the pier, though, and started to make her way over. She passed by a few fishermen who gave her strange looks, but she ignored them.

The end of the pier was empty, no one fishing there. She reached up and grabbed the railing, trying to scan the rippling water below. There were a few islands a few miles off in the distance, but otherwise the sea was empty.

Taylor sighed. She had hoped to catch Hensley in the act. But perhaps he would show up on his own accord, if he was the kidnapper.

Taylor went to turn around when she spotted a man walking up the pier with a fishing rod over his shoulder. He was wearing a bright yellow vest, and he looked vaguely familiar.

It was Alex Hensley.

Taylor’s heart rate picked up. She was going to get him. She'd finally found a lead.

Shaking from adrenaline, Taylor made her way over to him. He didn't notice her until she was right next to him. He looked up in surprise.

"What are you doing here?" he asked. "Did you come to fish too?"

"No," she said. "I came to talk to you."

His eyes widened, his internal alarm bells probably going off. Maybe he could smell that Taylor was with the law. "What? You can't do that. I'm busy."

"Can you spare a few minutes? I just need a quick word with you," Taylor said.

Hensley frowned. "I don't have time for this. I have to get some fish."

"You don't have time to talk to an FBI agent?" Taylor asked.

The color drained from Hensley's face.

Before Taylor could react, he dropped his gear and made a run for it.

CHAPTER TWENTY

Taylor chased after Hensley. The crowded pier was loud and chaotic, excited fishermen in yellow and green vests, with hats and sunglasses, shouting at each other over the loud waves rolling in on the shore. But Taylor didn't stop her pursuit. Just as she was about to grab him, he slipped between two fishermen and disappeared from sight.

"Wait!" she yelled. "Stop that man!"

Several fishermen looked at her, startled, but they didn't make a move to chase after him. She was on her own. He was swift and nimble—he dodged fishermen and jumped over the fishing nets that other people had placed in the way. Even though he was a middle-aged man, he was fast. Taylor had to run fast to catch up with him. The crowds of fishermen gasped and looked on with shock as the chase ensued.

In his haste, Hensley had lost his bucket hat, but Taylor still didn't have any luck grabbing him. He was moving too quickly for her to close the distance between them. She was running out of breath, but she didn't care. She couldn't let him get away.

"Stop!" she yelled. "I need to talk to you!"

Hensley didn't stop running up the pier, dodging past fishermen and their gear. Taylor was still too far away from him to reach out and grab him.

Taylor didn't know what to do—all she knew was that she needed to catch him. Without thinking, she swiped up a piece of heavy rope off the pier and threw it at Hensley. It caught onto his ankle—and caused him to fall right off the pier, into the water.

Hensley screamed as he fell into the water. Another fisherman, on the pier, saw him and immediately grabbed a pole, dropping his own fishing gear. He jumped over the railing and plunged into the water.

He pulled Hensley onto a boat. He was coughing and sputtering, his face pale.

Taylor ran over to the boat. "FBI! Move aside!"

The fisherman immediately released Hensley. Taylor slid in and jumped on him, slapping cuffs on his wrist, and began reading him his rights.

***

Taylor dragged Alex Hensley, dripping wet and stinking of fish, into the police station, immediately garnering confused looks from the staff. She was out of breath, but the adrenaline was pumping through her veins, making her feel almost invincible. It had worked—she had caught the kidnapper. At least, she hoped he was the guy.

She hauled him into an interrogation room and pushed him into a chair. She took a deep breath to calm herself. She turned to look at Hensley. He was slouching in his chair, his head low, his posture defeated.

"Where is she?" Taylor asked. "Where is Amy Schuler?"

"I don't know what you're talking about," he said.

Taylor placed her hands on the table and leaned forward. "Yes, you do. You kidnapped her, and you're going to tell me where you've taken her."

"I didn't kidnap anyone," Hensley said, scrambling. "You've got the wrong guy!"

Taylor took out her cell phone and showed him a picture of Amy. "What about her?"

Hensley looked at the picture. "I don't know her."

"Of course you know her." Taylor slammed her hands against the table.

"I don't know what you're talking about," Hensley said again. Taylor saw fear shining in his eyes.

"You took her from the beach," Taylor said. "Just like you assaulted that woman on the beach."

Hensley looked exhausted. "That was... I already did time for that, okay? I'm on parole, and I've been keeping my nose clean since. Look, you're crazy—I didn't kidnap anyone."

His use of the word 'crazy' made Taylor's hair stand on end. She wasn't crazy—but she was determined to convince herself this guy was the kidnapper. She had to believe it deep down in her gut.

She slammed her hands onto the table again. "You're going to tell me what happened to Amy Schuler. To Jessica Clements. To all the other girls you took." *And Angie,* Taylor thought desperately.

Hensley opened his mouth to reply when the door to the interrogation room flew open, and Sheriff Garth stormed in, Wesley behind him.

"What's going on here?" Garth demanded.

Taylor looked up at him, unsure of what to say. Did she dare tell him what was going on? How could she explain it?

"This woman kidnapped me!" Hensley said. "She's crazy! She's trying to frame me!"

Garth frowned and looked over at Taylor. "What is he talking about?"

"He's the kidnapper," Taylor said. "The person who has been kidnapping all those girls. Look—" She pointed at Hensley. "He was just trying to make a run for it. He's our guy."

Garth stared at her, then looked over at Hensley. Taylor saw something flicker in his eyes. Behind him, Wesley was giving Taylor a confused—and concerned—look. Did they not believe her?

"Special Agent Sage, let's talk in hall," Garth said.

Taylor had a bad feeling about this.

In the hallway, Taylor, Wesley, and Garth stood in a trifecta. Garth said, "Sage, there's no way Alex Hensley did it."

Taylor's stomach fell to the floor. "How do you know?"

"He wasn't even on the island the night Amy Schuler went missing. I know because he reported that he was visiting family to me. Every time he leaves the island, it's gotta be recorded—it's part of his parole. I confirmed with the ferry that he left that day and came back the next."

Taylor felt so sick she could hardly speak. She was wrong. Again. This was another dead end. "Why wasn't that in the report, Sheriff?" She felt embarrassed, and like crap. She'd just exploded on that guy.

"I didn't think it was relevant," Garth said.

"If that's the case," Wesley said," then he couldn't have kidnapped Amy."

Taylor's mouth went dry. She felt like she couldn't breathe. "Then why did he run from me?"

"He probably panicked," Garth said. "The guy's been doing everything he can to stay clean and avoid going back to jail. Special Agent Sage, I'm sorry, but you're wrong on this one."

Taylor turned and looked out the window. There was a sense of defeat in her bones. She saw a lone seagull on the horizon, flying in the wind.

"I was wrong," she murmured. "I was so sure. He was the right guy."

"I'll go in there and clean up this mess," Garth said, glaring at Taylor and Wesley. "You two sort out what you're really doing on this island."

Taylor didn't want to be in this police station for another minute. She stormed out, into the hot and humid day. Taylor's mouth was a desert and her tongue felt dry. The sun shining above disoriented her. In her hallucination, the sun was a bloated, sickly orange ball, with cracks and fissures spider-webbing across the surface. She was ringed with fire and lit like a cauldron, and gave off no heat, only a chalky ash taste in her mouth.

In all honesty, Taylor felt like she was losing her mind.

Wesley stormed out of the station after her. "Sage!"

She snapped back to reality and faced her partner.

"What's going on with you?" Wesley demanded. "What made you so sure that was the guy? And why the hell didn't you tell me?"

Taylor averted her eyes. "He'd been charged with assault before, and..."

"If you'd just talked to me then we could've sorted it out with Garth before going in guns blazing. For fuck's sake, Sage..." Wesley's brows pinched as he looked away. "I'm getting worried about you. You're not yourself."

Taylor turned away. He was right. But she didn't want to admit it.

"I should have talked to you," she said, "but I was worried you'd shut me down."

She thought back to the real lead she'd discovered earlier, before she got distracted with Alex Hensley. The gap tooth detail. The Hensley thing had nothing to do with that—Taylor had just lost herself in the idea of him being the kidnapper, but Wesley had a point. She wasn't herself, and she needed to be more open with her partner.

"Look," she said, "the Hensley thing—I messed up. I admit it. But there's more work to do; I noticed another similarity between all the girls and—"

Taylor's phone began ringing in her pocket. She looked up at Wesley to see nothing but pity on his face, and frankly, it pissed Taylor off. She took out her phone and saw it was Winchester.

"It's the chief," she muttered. "I gotta take this."

Taylor stepped off to the side, away from Wesley's ears, and turned away. The sun beat down on her. She accepted the call and pressed the phone to her ear.

"Chief—"

"Sage," Winchester said, "I hope you know what the hell you're doing."

Taylor paused. She wasn't ready for this conversation.

"Wesley let me in on the case," he said. "How'd you even end up on Brock Island, of all places?"

Taylor couldn't tell him the truth—at best, he'd think she was insane. At worst, she'd be seen as unfit for her job. And if Taylor was ever fired from the FBI, she had no idea what she'd do.

"Chief..." Taylor sighed, trying to think of a way out of this. "I should've called you sooner, but I got caught up. I need you to trust me. I've had a solid track record so far, right?"

A pause on the other end, before Winchester said, "Damn right, but Wesley's expressed some concern for your mental health."

Taylor glanced over her shoulder at Wesley, who was typing on his phone in front of the police station.

"What did he say?" she asked.

"He's got this idea in his head that you think this case is somehow linked to your missing sister," Chief said, and it was sobering to hear it said out loud, from his mouth. "I told him that's crazy talk. Your sister went missing two decades ago. There's no way you'd be thinking this random case is somehow connected."

Taylor didn't know what to say, so she went with nothing. But inside, anger curled at her. Wesley didn't need to tell Winchester, to make it all personal. She'd trusted him with that information about Angie and he'd thrown away that trust. Maybe it was done out of care for her—but Taylor wished he'd talked to her about it before telling Winchester.

She felt even more deep shame and confusion. She stopped to consider everything she'd done in the past forty-eight hours. Seeing Ben move out had made their divorce all too real. Her father's heart attack. Coming to this island on little more than a hunch, certain she'd get an answer about Angie...

Taylor had to ask herself: What *was* she really doing here now? Of course it had been to find Angie, but had she really attached herself to this case, lost her sanity in it? In her right mind, she never would have attacked Garrett Smith like she had yesterday.

One thing was certain. There were girls going missing on this island, and Taylor had to focus on that.

"I'm sorry for not calling you sooner, Chief," she said to Winchester. "I really just want to find out what happened to these girls."

"Well, I won't stop you," Winchester said. "But you need to take care of yourself."

There was a beat of silence. Taylor didn't know what to say to that.

"Good luck," he said, and hung up.

That was that.

Taylor's head pounded as she went back to face Wesley. He put his phone away and met her eyes.

"Everything okay?"

Taylor decided not to bring up the fact that she knew Wesley had told Winchester about Angie. It didn't matter now, and she knew they were right to worry about her. Taylor made a silent vow to keep her head on straight, forget about Angie and the symbols and all of that, and try to find those missing girls.

"Yeah, it's all good," Taylor said. "I wanted to tell you, I noticed that all the missing girls have a slight gap between their front teeth, even Amy Schuler. Which means every one of them had brown hair, light eyes, and a slight gap tooth."

Wesley stroked his hand over his five o-clock shadow. "That seems significant for sure," he said. "What do you think it means?"

Taylor took a moment to consider the profile rationally. If he was taking women that all have similar features, then it seemed likely he was perhaps taking them because they reminded him of someone else. An ex-girlfriend, maybe. A wife. A sister. Mother. It could be anyone.

"I think he's chasing somebody he used to know," Taylor told Wesley. "He's trying to replace a woman in his life, probably one who left him or died."

"A solid theory," Wesley said. "But I have no clue where to go from here."

The gears in Taylor's head were turning. She felt like she'd sobered up, like she could think clearly again. "We could look into women who've died on the island, maybe in the last year or so, see if anyone looks like the missing girls."

"Good idea. Let's start—"

Suddenly, Garth burst out of the station, looking frazzled. Taylor and Wesley stood at attention, and he looked at them with a sigh.

"Good. You two are still here."

"What's going on?" Taylor asked.

Garth took a breath. "We've got another missing girl."

CHAPTER TWENTY ONE

Taylor's heart stopped when she and Wesley pulled up to a familiar street on Brock Island, having borrowed one of the police cars. Wesley was behind the wheel, and they'd been quiet the whole way here. But as they drew near, Taylor could feel that Wesley was thinking the same thing as her.

This was the same street they were on yesterday, when they came to question Randy and his daughter, Katelyn.

"Tell me it wasn't her," Taylor said.

But they stopped outside of the exact same house where yesterday, Katelyn and her dad had been washing the car. Taylor thought about the girl. If she was remembering right—Katelyn did have a slight gap tooth, just like Amy, just like the other girls. And she had dark hair too.

She would fit the profile perfectly.

Taylor and Wesley hurried out of the car, up to the front door of the house, and knocked. Moments later, Randy, looking shaken-up, answered.

"Oh, thank God you're here," he said. "Come in."

Inside, the house was part modern, part cottage. The living room had a faux-brick fireplace, complete with a roaring fire. The room was decorated with long, thick, navy carpet, and a giant flat screen TV in front of the fireplace. It was quiet, except for the ticking of a clock. It was a soft tick, and the house was so silent that it seemed to be in slow motion.

"My other two are at school right now," Randy said. "But Katelyn—she never showed up to class."

Taylor looked at the walls. There were photos of two little boys, and then Katelyn, smiling, gap toothed and all.

"Sheriff Garth said you declared her as missing, even though it hasn't been twenty-four hours," Wesley said to Randy.

Randy had the eyes of a desperate father. "Yes, but she isn't at school. She isn't anywhere. And what's even weirder is that she left her phone in her room."

"Her room?" Wesley asked. "Do you think it's possible she just went somewhere, and didn't tell you?"

Randy sighed. "No, there's no way. Katelyn would never take off without telling me. Never."

Taylor's breath caught in her throat. She and Wesley exchanged a worried look.

"When did you see her last?" Wesley asked.

"This morning. We went out early for breakfast with one of her friends, walked along the pier for a bit, then came home to get ready for school. I thought Katelyn had left, but then I got a call from the school hours later saying she never showed up for class. I thought maybe she was skipping, so I went into her room, and that's when I found the phone and called the police." Once more, his eyes were desperate. "You have to believe me. She isn't like this."

Wesley turned to Taylor, who picked up where he left off.

"Do you know if Katelyn was seeing anyone?" she asked Randy. "A boyfriend? An ex? Anything like that?"

"She wasn't seeing anyone from school, if that's what you mean," Randy said. "Sheriff Garth thinks I'm jumping the gun on this, and that Katelyn is just off with a friend somewhere, but you don't understand—she isn't like this. She never misses school. And she'd never leave without her phone."

Taylor nodded. Randy was doing the right thing—in fact, she was certain his gut instinct was spot on.

"With the girls going missing," Taylor said, "I'm glad you called it in right away. We should take a look at Katelyn's room and see if we can find anything. She might be fine, but it's worth looking into."

Randy put a hand to his face and then led the way to Katelyn's room. "It's up here," he said.

The upstairs of the house was all bedrooms—three to be exact. One of them was Randy's, and the other two were for his three children.

Katelyn's room was the second one on the right. Her door was open, and Taylor and Wesley stepped in. The walls were covered with posters of singers and actors, the obligatory unicorn on the wall, and then a bunch of clothes, books, and shoes all strewn across the floor.

It was messy, but Taylor didn't see anything out of the ordinary.

"Is this her phone?" Taylor asked, pointing to a pink phone on the floor.

"Yes," Randy said. "I tried calling it, but it goes right to voicemail."

Wesley picked it up, and entered a passcode, which was something like 111111. Maybe that was his daughter's simple code and he was trying it out. But it didn't work.

"You know the password?" Wesley asked.

"No," Randy said. "I trust Kate. She has freedom."

"What about her social media?" Taylor asked. "Do you have her password for that?"

Randy shook his head. "I tried all of the ones I know, but nothing is working. That's why I called the police. I was getting worried."

Wesley gave Taylor a look, and she knew what he was thinking. Was there any way to access Katelyn's social media remotely? Could they get into her account from a computer and find her? Of course, that would only help if Katelyn was off with a friend.

The closet door, cracked and open. The hangers on the closet's racks were filled to the brim with different outfits.

"What was Katelyn wearing when you saw her last?" Taylor asked.

"A striped dress, this morning," Randy said. "Please, you have to find her..."

"We believe you," Wesley assured. "We just want to get all the facts right."

Randy nodded. "I know. And I just... I just feel helpless and scared. I don't know where she is."

Wesley ran his hand through his hair and sighed. "We'll do everything we can to find Katelyn," he said.

Randy took a shuddering breath. "Thank you," he said. "I moved here to escape the chaos of the city, and I never thought something like this could happen in a place like this..."

As Wesley and Randy talked, Taylor tuned out of the conversation. She walked over to the bedroom window and peeked down, into the backyard.

The backyard was a well-tended oasis, green with grass and trees and flowers, sun shining down the white walls on the outside of the house. The light danced through the blades of grass and reflected in the fountain.

But that wasn't all. The house faced against a small patch of forest. Some of the grass looked trampled—like someone had walked through it.

Part of Taylor wanted to point it out to Wesley. She wanted to suggest that Katelyn could have been abducted by a stranger and dragged off into the woods. But she couldn't do it in front of Randy.

Taylor faced the other two. "Why don't you show us the rest of the house, Randy?" she asked. "So we can see if anything is missing."

Randy nodded. "Of course. I'm so sorry—I'm just so frazzled right now. I don't know what to do."

Randy led the agents downstairs, and the three of them stood in the foyer. The stairs were steep and spiral, and Wesley had to duck so he could walk down them comfortably.

"This is a lovely home," Wesley said, trying to make conversation. "You've done a good job raising your kids."

"Thank you," Randy said. "It's been hard work, but I've loved every minute of it."

"Randy," Taylor cut in, wanting a minute alone with Wesley, "would you mind grabbing us one of Katelyn's yearbooks? It will be helpful for us to know as much about her as possible."

Wesley shot Taylor a confused look, but Randy disappeared into the living room.

Taylor looked up at him. "I noticed some damaged grass in the back, maybe a trail," she whispered. "I want to go check it out, but I don't want to freak him out."

Wesley nodded. "I can keep talking to him, see what else I can learn about Katelyn. But be careful."

"Thanks."

Randy came back into the foyer holding the book. Taylor gave him a smile. "Special Agent Wesley will take care of you from here, Randy," Taylor said. "I'm going to see what I can find out about Katelyn in town."

"Thank you," Randy said. "And be careful. I'm worried."

She turned and walked out of the house, but as soon as she was out, she made a beeline for the back, slipping on her sunglasses to protect her eyes from the sun.

The grass in the back was trampled, as Taylor had suspected. It was thin and dry, so it was easy to follow the trail into the woods. Taylor paused, looking around to see if there were any trails that matched the exit in the back of the house, but there was nothing.

"Damn," she whispered.

She had to follow the trail, or she wouldn't be able to find the source of the trampled grass. But the more she followed, the sparser the trail became.

Taylor found herself walking through the sparse forest. The trees were bare, whipped by wind and sun, the dried leaves crackled under the weight her shoes. The ground was cushioned by old leaves. The scent of desiccated grasses mixed with the smell of dying leaves and the smell of the forest and beach.

Suddenly, something up ahead caught Taylor's eye. It gleamed in the sunlight. She snapped on a glove, bent down, and picked it up.

It was a piece of a fishing line with a small lure attached to the end, an orange fish with a green line on it.

This could belong to anyone. Fishing was common on the island, after all, but it was worth keeping, just in case. Taylor pulled an evidence bag from her pocket and put in the line, then removed her glove.

Taylor kept moving, even though she'd lost the trail. Eventually, she found herself back on a suburban street. Taylor looked around, not just at the houses, but at the people too. She noted the rich clothes, the manicured lawns, the cars that appeared to be new. Everyone looked prosperous and happy. In the distance, off the coastline, was what looked like an old water mill with a wheel attached. There was the sound of waves crashing against the shore. The sound of cars driving by. Small children laughing and running.

No sign of Katelyn, and no sign of the kidnapper.

Taylor paused. She'd been so sure that was a trail back there, but was she seeing things again?

Taylor kept walking along the street, as though she were nothing but a regular pedestrian, and tried to think deeper. She didn't know enough about this person's mental state to understand why he might be doing this. He had to be chasing someone, like she'd theorized before. But even if that were the case, why did he take so many girls?

And where did he keep them?

Were they even alive?

The thought made Taylor's skin crawl. By statistics alone, it was unlikely most of the missing girls were still alive. For Katelyn and Amy, there was hope, but the rest had been missing for too long.

Just like Angie.

Taylor didn't want to think about that. She shook the thoughts from her head, just as she looked up at the mid-morning sky. Above the tops of the houses, she made out the wheel.

To her right, there was a convenience store mixed in with all the houses. The door was open, giving Taylor a view inside.

And at the front there was a box of tarot cards for sale.

CHAPTER TWENTY TWO

Taylor sat on a picnic table in the middle of a park, holding her new pack of tarot cards, but she hadn't opened them yet. The box was purple with gold embossed on it, and it reminded her so much of Belasco.

She couldn't waste much time doing this. But the temptation to try had been too real. Taylor was stuck, and she needed answers. Maybe this was stupid—but maybe, just maybe, it could help.

Taylor had spent the last couple minutes learning online how to perform a tarot reading on herself. She took the cards out and began shuffling them. She tried not to think about the absurdity of what she was doing, and instead focused on getting the cards absolutely perfect in her hand. She'd figure out the method later. For now, she just needed the perfect cards.

After she felt satisfied, Taylor cut the deck and drew three cards, placing them face down in a row. She closed her eyes and took a deep breath. Taylor's mind rested in a place of calm, a place of peace. She felt the vibrations and pulses of life around her, and she let it enter her, soothe her, and ease the ache in her head.

She flipped the first card over, and saw it was The Lovers.

The card showed two people in an embrace, their hair long and wild, the sun behind them. Taylor didn't know what this could mean: what lovers?

She flipped the next card. It was the Ten of Swords.

The ten of swords was an image of a man crossing a beach, his face hidden by a hood. His body was draped in a cloak made of ten swords, and his feet were bare, walking across the sand. The image of his feet reminded Taylor of the girls. He was being led. The swords were a symbol of pain, and the beach was a sign of rebirth.

Taylor wondered what it meant. Was her interpretation wrong? She wished Belasco was here to tell her what it all meant, but she was left playing a guessing game.

The last card Taylor flipped up was The Wheel of Fortune.

It was a picture of an elaborate wheel. The wheel had a top half, with angels and demons, and a bottom half, with a group of people. The wheel was turning, as though it might fly off at any second. The wheel was black and white, but in the background, there were hints of several other images. One was a rainbow. Another was a crescent moon.

There was a story in this card; Taylor knew that. But it was confusing, and it didn't give her any answers. She was beginning to doubt the wisdom of this.

But something about that wheel struck a familiar chord with her. Then, it hit her like a ton of bricks—the water wheel she'd seen off the coastline.

Taylor gathered up the cards and put them away, sticking them in her pocket, then hurried out of the park, back to the street. Since the suburb was elevated, it gave a view of the coastline in the distance—and the wheel.

Taylor hurried there, her heart in her throat.

***

The building was an abandoned mill, made of old, decaying brick that stood out against the blue ocean behind it. Attached to its side was the water wheel, full of algae and plant life; clearly, it had not turned in years.

Taylor stopped to think about her plan of action. Now that she was staring this place down, it felt real. She didn't know what she'd find here—if anything—but if this was where the cards were pointing, it had to be worth checking out.

There was an old, rusted door that led inside the building. Above the door, there was a rusted metal sign that read NO TRESPASSING.

Taylor tried the handle, but it was locked. She sighed, then took out her lock picks, and went to work.

Once she was inside, Taylor had to stop and let her eyes adjust. The building was dark, and there was nothing but sunlight coming through the door. And inside, there was an overwhelming musk of rot and decay, as though the place had been left to itself for years.

Taylor looked around. She saw a stairwell going up, and another leading down to a lower level. There was no power. The building was quiet, save for the occasional squeak of a floorboard. The walls were covered in graffiti. It was dark, but there was enough ambient light to make out what it said.

Never forget.

Beware the lighthouse.

The worst is yet to come.

You are here.

Taylor swept her flashlight across the wall and started reading the letters. Taylor shuddered. She didn't know what this stuff was about, but she didn't like it. Faintly, there was a scent in the air, almost like charcoal, and it stung her eyes, almost like tear gas. Taylor looked down at the floor. There was a trail of black soot. It looked like it had been there for years.

Taylor looked back at the wall, and saw the letters were written backwards.

Don't trust the water.

She took the stairs going up, as they seemed more likely to lead to the roof. As she ascended, she felt herself having to hold on to the railing. The wood was frail and worn, and felt like it would snap with just a little more pressure. She reached the top and pulled open the door.

It opened out to a wooden deck, with an old rusty railing. There was a view to the sky, but Taylor had a feeling that wasn't what the place was built for. From here, it looked like you could see the water wheel. But there was no water in it now. Just a bunch of algae and green plants.

Taylor walked to the edge and looked down.

There was nothing here.

Feeling defeated, Taylor made her way back to the main level. Another waste of time. Another dead end.

But just then—a noise. Like somebody moving.

Taylor shone her flashlight in the back corner of the room.

A man, hidden underneath a blanket, squinted back at her.

"Hello?" Taylor asked.

The man got up, and shambled out into the light. He was an old man, balding, and covered in age spots. He looked ill, and his eyes looked dead.

"Who are you?" Taylor asked.

The man didn't answer. He moved closer.

"Who are you?" Taylor asked again, her pulse pounding.

But the man just stumbled up to her.

"Help," he croaked out—but he was coming right at Taylor with open arms.

She didn't know what to do. Was he going to attack her? She considered her gun. Could this be the kidnapper?

Could the girls be here?

Before she could react, the man lunged at her. Taylor shouted and stumbled back. As she did, her feet slipped in the dust and she fell. Before she could react, the man had landed on top of her. She pushed him off, tried to scoot away. His hands were on her, and he grunted.

Taylor swung her flashlight again. The man grabbed it, and it slipped from her fingers. She tried to get up, but the man grabbed her by the wrist and pulled her back.

Panic flooded over her. She shouted again, but the man was on top of her, and he had her pinned. A strong odor surrounded her, and Taylor wanted to be sick.

With all her might, she kneed him in the groin, and he finally fell off her. Taylor stood up immediately and whipped her gun out, pointing it right at him. The man cowered on the ground with his hands up.

"Where are the girls?" Taylor exclaimed.

"Girls!" He started laughing, wheezy and throaty, making Taylor's blood boil. "Girls, girls, girls," he said, "it's all about the girls."

Was this the kidnapper? Had he been here the whole time? Taylor was aghast.

"Where are they?" she demanded.

"Girls everywhere," he said, laughing.

Taylor stopped and looked at this man. Really looked. But then he started to laugh again, and Taylor was confused. This wasn't right. The man didn't seem right. What was happening here? She tried to reason with him.

"Where are the girls?" she asked again.

But he'd gone catatonic. This person was clearly unwell. Maybe unwell enough to have taken the girls. She lifted him by his arm and herded him out the door.

"You're coming with me," she said.

If this man was their kidnapper, maybe she could get answers out of him. Maybe she could track the girls. Maybe she could find them.

Taylor dragged him down the stairs, with him laughing the whole way. She wasn't sure what to think, but she was going to get some answers.

CHAPTER TWENTY THREE

Taylor dragged the homeless man into the station, where Officer Brady hurried out of his office and spotted them.

"Holy crap," he said, "is that Wilson?"

The homeless man—Wilson, apparently—was still laughing and muttering like a maniac, even as Taylor had him cuffed. He'd been incoherent the entire trip here, and Taylor's patience was running thin.

"You know this dirtbag?" Taylor asked Brady.

"Yeah, we know him well here," Brady said, "but we haven't seen him in months. We thought he left the island."

"So he's not dangerous, then?" Taylor asked.

Brady seemed to ponder this, running his hand along his chin. "He's homeless," Brady said, "and he's been known to break into places and steal food and things, but he doesn't seem like the kind of guy who'd kidnap girls."

"That's not a guarantee," Taylor said, "I've seen plenty of guys on the street that seemed perfectly normal, and they go home to beat their wives and molest their kids."

"You've got a point," Brady said.

Taylor dragged Wilson, still muttering obscenities, toward the interrogation room down the hall. She shoved him into the room and slammed the door behind them. Wilson looked around, confused. His hair was auburn and frazzled, and his long beard looked like it hadn't seen a wash in years. His eyeballs were blank and buggy, like he had no idea what planet he was on.

"Sit," Taylor said.

"Huh?" Wilson started thrashing again when he realized he was cuffed. Taylor just shoved him onto the chair, and thankfully, he stayed put.

He didn't seem to be able to focus. This was not a normal human.

"Who are you?" Taylor asked.

But Wilson was too incoherent to answer. He kept thrashing around, and trying to get up, but Taylor kept shoving him back down.

"Sit!" she exclaimed.

Finally, Wilson seemed to calm down, and he sort of noticed Taylor.

"Who?" he asked.

"My name is Special Agent Taylor Sage of the FBI," Taylor said, "and you are?" She wasn't confident he would even know his own name.

"No," Wilson said, "I'm Wilson. Wilson Wilson..."

Taylor didn't have time for whatever game he was playing. "Where's Katelyn, Wilson?" she asked. "Where's Amy Schuler?"

"Who?" He looked at her, his face twisted, completely perplexed.

In truth, Taylor didn't know how to handle this. She had never come face-to-face with somebody so... incoherent before. Was he really capable of orchestrating a plan to kidnap those girls? And if he did, where were they? If he killed them, he would have had to hide the bodies somewhere, but the abandoned mill was empty.

Doubt began to grow inside her, but she pushed on.

"Where were you this morning, Wilson?"

"Sleep, sleep," he said.

Suddenly, a knock at the door. Taylor looked over her shoulder to see Wesley coming in. He took in the man in front of Taylor and raised his eyebrows.

"Special Agent Wesley," Taylor said, "I'm glad you could join us."

Wilson looked at Wesley, bug-eyed, as he took the seat beside Taylor. Taylor and Wesley exchanged a glance before Taylor picked the interrogation back up. She needed to try a gentler approach to get this guy talking.

"Where do you live, Wilson?" Taylor asked. "Are you always at the abandoned mill?"

Wilson looked back and forth from Taylor to Wesley. "Where?" he asked.

"What do you do there?" Taylor asked.

"Sleep," Wilson said.

"What do you do in the daytime?" Wesley asked.

Wilson pointed at Wesley. "Wesley," he said.

"You just stay at the mill?" Taylor asked.

"Yes," Wilson said, "but I don't hurt anyone. I don't steal. I don't do anything wrong."

"What do you do when you're not at the mill?" Taylor asked.

"Mill," Wilson said, "sleep, mill."

"Who do you talk to?" Wesley asked.

"Nobody," Wilson said. "Nobody."

This was going nowhere. Taylor sighed. Okay then. Another approach. She took out her phone and pulled up a picture of Katelyn, then showed it to Wilson, who just looked at the photo like he was completely bamboozled.

"Do you know this girl, Wilson?" Taylor asked.

"Wow, she is pretty," he said.

"Do you know her?" Taylor repeated, her voice firm. Wilson didn't answer, so she swiped to a photo of Amy. "What about her, Wilson? Have you seen her?"

"Pretty girl," Wilson said.

"Do you know her?" Taylor was seriously losing her patience.

Wilson looked at all the pictures on the phone, then shook his head. "No," he said, "no."

"Bullshit. Where are those girls, Wilson?" Taylor asked.

"Go," Wilson said, "go."

Taylor gave a heavy sigh. This wasn't working. She was going to have to change tactics and come at this from a different angle.

"Where do you come from, Wilson?" Taylor asked. "Do you have a family? Do you have friends? Or do you just sleep alone at the mill?"

"Family," Wilson said, "no friends, family."

"Your family is on the island?" Taylor asked.

"My family is the island," Wilson said, "the island is my family."

Frustrated, Taylor stood up. This wasn't working. "Wait here, Wilson," Taylor said. "We'll be right back."

With that, Taylor and Wesley left the interrogation room and reconvened in the hallway. Taylor looked up at Wesley, who still had that concerned look on his face.

"How'd you find this guy?" he asked.

"Trail sort of led to the abandoned mill," Taylor muttered, obviously not willing to admit it was the tarot cards that led her there. "I mostly went there on a hunch, and found him."

"Any other evidence of the girls there?"

"Not that I could see," Taylor said. "But he could easily be our guy. He has no alibi. And he's clearly delusional."

"Can't deny that one," Wesley said. He stuffed his hands in his pockets. "This could be our guy, Sage."

"I think he is."

It was almost underwhelming. Maybe Taylor had pictured more of a criminal mastermind, not this deranged and unwell man. But as long as no more girls were hurt, that was all she cared about.

But of course, the most important question now was—where were the girls he'd already taken?

Were they still alive?

"I'm gonna go back in there and see if I can get him to talk," Taylor said. "Maybe you can find out where Garth is and run the whole thing by him. Wilson's known to the force here."

"Sounds good," Wesley said. "And good luck."

Taylor took a deep breath and faced the door to the interrogation room, praying she could finally get some answers for the families of these girls. She went back in, where Wilson was still sitting in the chair—but this time, he was looking around the room, seeming more aware of his surroundings.

"Where am I?" he asked, his eyes on Taylor. "How'd I get here?"

Taylor frowned as she sat down. "You don't remember, Wilson?"

"Oh, God, what'd I do? How'd I get here?"

Taylor paused. Was this all an act? It didn't seem like one, but it only confused her more. He seemed to be experiencing a moment of lucidity, but how?

"Wilson, I just want to ask you some more questions, if that's okay," Taylor said. "You do remember me, right? Taylor. Special Agent Sage."

"Agent?" Wilson asked. "What's happening?"

"Where are you from, Wilson?" Taylor asked. "Do you know?"

Wilson just stared at her for a minute, his face completely empty. Then, abruptly, he grinned. "I'm from the island," he said. "The island is my home."

"What island would that be?" Taylor asked.

"This island," Wilson said, seemingly perplexed by her question. "Where I was born. My home. Brock Island."

"Okay, good," Taylor said. "We're on Brock Island now." She pulled out her phone and opened the photo of Katelyn again and showed it to Wilson. "Do you recognize this girl?"

"I've never seen her in my life," Wilson said.

Taylor flipped to the next photo of Amy. "What about her?"

Wilson shook his head. His eyes landed on Taylor, desperate. "Please. I don't know how I got here. I've never seen those girls. What is going on?"

"I brought you here, Wilson," Taylor said. "I found you sleeping in the abandoned mill, and you attacked me."

"I did? I'm sorry! I didn't—I wasn't—"

"It's okay," Taylor said, to keep him calm. "I'm not hurt. But I need to know where the girls are."

"What girls? I don't know them!" Wilson said. "I haven't seen them; I've never seen them before."

"Do you know where any of the girls on this island are?" Taylor asked.

"I don't know any girls. I'm not allowed to talk to girls."

"What do you mean?" Taylor asked. "Who told you that?"

Wilson was shaking his head. He was distressed, but he didn't seem to be lying. "I'm not allowed to talk to girls," he repeated. "It's a sin. I'm not allowed."

"Who told you that?" Taylor asked. "Who told you it's a sin to talk to girls?"

"My father," Wilson said, looking at the ground, as though ashamed. "My father told me that. I went away in the mill to hide, to stay away. I've never taken anybody, I promise..."

Taylor was left speechless. She didn't know what to tell Wilson. This was beyond anything she had ever seen before. But she could see it in this man's eyes: he was telling the truth. He wasn't who Taylor was looking for; he was just an ill man who needed help, who needed mental health treatment.

She couldn't know for sure. It was true; he clearly had no alibi, and if he was this unwell, maybe he did hurt them... but Taylor felt it in her core that he wasn't capable of this plot.

Damn, Taylor thought. If that were the case, then Wilson was innocent—and the real kidnapper was still out there.

Head reeling, Taylor stood up. "Okay, Wilson, we're going to keep you here for a bit until we figure things out, okay?"

"What happened? Did I do something wrong? Is it okay if I stay in the mill? I promise I won't hurt anybody. I just need to stay there, away from people. Please."

"It's fine, Wilson," Taylor said. "It's okay for now. We'll let you know when we figure out what we're doing next."

"I'm sorry," Wilson said, his voice breaking. "I'm sorry, I really am."

Taylor just nodded and left the interrogation room. She stood in the hallway for a moment, wondering what to do next. All of these threads;

they had to mean something, right? Taylor found herself still clinging onto hope that the cards had meant something, but if Wilson was innocent, then it was another dead end.

Then, she remembered: the evidence bag in her pocket.

Taylor pulled out the fishing line and lure. It was thin, nondescript, and not unique by any means. The lure itself seemed like a generic fish shape. But Taylor didn't know anything about fishing.

Besides, this might not mean anything. Taylor remembered her earlier plan—to check the obituaries of any women who'd died before the girls started going missing.

Taylor went and sat in the waiting room, taking out her phone. Maybe it was a longshot, but…

Taylor looked at the obits. She flipped through them, her eyes scanning over the names as fast as she could. Bethany Shipman, killed in a motorcycle accident. Mary Jones, heart attack. Paul Valdez, slipped off a cliff. And...

Taylor's blood ran cold.

She looked at the obituary once more, and her heart sank. It was an old black and white photo of a dark-haired woman in her youth, wearing a striped dress. She had light eyes—and a slight gap between her front teeth.

Patricia Marie Gable.

She'd died at sixty-eight, just last year. Cancer. She left behind no children, but one husband:

Robert Gable.

CHAPTER TWENTY FOUR

The bait and tackle shop was devoid of customers when Taylor entered. A flood of odor followed her through the door, from the tanks to the counters, from the hooks and other fishing paraphernalia to the cash register to the greasy knives and buckets of bait on the cabinets, and back again. The fishy and chemical scented odor clung to Taylor's skin, perfumed the air, and stunk of death to her nose.

Robert Gable knelt down beside a display rack and was hanging up items on the shelves when Taylor entered, the door dinging behind her. He looked up, confused, and stood at attention. He was wearing overalls and muddy boots, his beer belly tucked beneath.

"You again," he said. "The FBI agent, right?"

Taylor paused. She'd never identified herself to Robert earlier.

As though he caught on, he said, "I saw the chase of Hensley earlier. Heard you yelling FBI."

"Ah." Taylor nodded, eyeing him. "Yes, Hensley was taken in."

"What'd he do?"

"I'm afraid I can't say." Taylor rifled in her pocket for the lure and pulled it out, then showed it to Robert. "Actually, I'm here looking for information. Do you recognize this lure?"

It was just an excuse to get him talking. But Taylor was keeping her eyes firm on him.

Robert eyed Taylor, then the lure in the evidence bag. He let out a gruff grunt. "We sell them here," he said simply.

"Do you happen to know who could have bought this one?"

"No idea," he said. "It's a generic. There are tons." He gestured to the wall of lures. "You can check if you want." Robert eyed her with suspicion. "What's going on?"

Taylor paused. Everything in her gut was telling her that something was seriously off with this guy. She had no proof currently that he was the right one—but she had a damn strong hunch.

"I'm sorry for bothering you," Taylor said. "Just trying to follow up on some leads."

"You got leads?" Robert asked. "I didn't know there was a case. I thought it was all solved. You arrested Henley."

"No, there's definitely a case," Taylor said, her unease growing stronger at the bait shop owner's confusion. "I'm sure you've heard of the girls going missing on the island."

Robert's eyes, which were dark green like sea water, flashed. "I heard about that, yeah."

Taylor could feel her alarm bells going off. To seem casual, she glanced around the shop, her hands in her pockets, and asked, "How long have you lived here, Mr. Gable?"

"About fifteen years," he said.

"Do you like it here?"

"I'm not sure I understand what you mean. Why do you keep asking me all these questions?"

"I'm just trying to get a feel for the island," Taylor said. "It seems quiet."

"It is. That's why I like it. I like quiet. I like peaceful."

"There's a surprising amount of crime here, though," Taylor said. "I saw that the police are stretched thin. It must be hard for you, running a business like this."

"I'm not worried about myself," Robert said. "I can take care of myself. I don't have kids or anything, but I have friends. I can handle it. I've done this for years."

Taylor watched him as he spoke. He had no emotion in his eyes. He was quiet, almost robotic.

"It must be hard, being so isolated here," Taylor said. "How do you pass the time?"

"I fish," Robert said, surprised. "All the time. That's how I relax. Haven't you seen all the fish?"

Taylor turned, and saw the fish. There were at least two large, full-sized fish in a tank on the counter. Taylor whistled. "Wow. Those are some big ones. Must have taken you a long time to catch them."

"It did," Robert said, a smile curling the corner of his lips. "They're the biggest ones I've ever caught. It gives me something to work toward."

"That's dedication. You must really like being here."

"I told you; I like quiet." Robert's tone was dull.

Taylor remembered the photo of Robert and a woman behind the cash register.

"And do you have a wife?" Taylor asked.

"I did," Robert said. "She died."

Taylor met Robert's gaze, which was firm on hers. His posture was rigid.

"I'm so sorry," Taylor said. "When did that happen?"

"Last year," he said.

She wandered over to the cash counter, and Robert followed.

"You looking for something to buy now?" he asked, his voice suspicious.

But Taylor was already at the counter. There was the back door she'd noticed earlier, still closed, and then the photo of Robert and the woman.

Taylor got a closer look.

The woman had dark hair, light eyes, and a slight gap in her tooth. This was definitely the young version of the woman she'd seen online. And she looked so similar to the missing girls that it made Taylor's stomach roll.

Maybe this was what the cards had been trying to tell her when she drew The Lovers. Robert and his wife, Patricia—it was them.

It took everything in Taylor to keep her cool. She couldn't react, not yet. She needed more.

She needed to know what was behind the door leading to the back.

She faced Robert, who was still watching her like a hawk. Taylor motioned to the photo behind the cash register. "Your wife. She looks nice. You looked happy together."

"Yeah," Robert said, his tone gruff and tense.

"How did she die?"

Robert's face turned to stone and his eyes darkened. "Cancer took her."

"I'm sorry." She faced the back room door again, then asked, "What's in the back room, Mr. Gable?"

"Nothing," he said, his voice robotic. "Just storage. Bags of bait, stuff like that. Nothing for you to worry about. I think that's all you need."

Something about his tone sent a chill up Taylor's spine. She knew it wasn't nothing. Her alarm bells were blaring in her head, telling her she had to get behind that door. She had to know what was back there. But Robert was showing no signs of letting her in.

Taylor steeled herself. She was a federal agent. She could do this.

"Mr. Gable, I'm sorry to disturb your work, but I'm going to have to ask you to step aside."

Taylor took a step toward the door, but Robert caught her hand.

"I said, that's it," he growled.

"Let go of me," Taylor said, her voice low and threatening. She met his gaze, and his eyes widened. Taylor yanked her hand away.

She stepped toward the door, but Robert blocked her way, his arms crossed over his chest.

"I'm not letting you back there," he snarled.

Taylor raised her hands up, keeping her distance. She eyed Robert, and then asked, "Did your wife work here, too?"

Robert's eyes flickered for a split second, but other than that, his face was stoic.

"Yes," he said.

"I need to see what's in the back room, Mr. Gable."

"I've told you what's back there," he said, his voice low and threatening. "Nothing but bags of bait."

Taylor eyed him. His tone was off. He was hiding something.

"I'm sorry, Mr. Gable. If you refuse to let me see what's behind that door, I'm going to have to insist that we go down to the station together."

Robert's eyes narrowed. His voice was level. "I'm trying to be reasonable here," he said. "I don't want to make a scene."

"Then you'll let me see what's behind the door," Taylor said.

Robert's eyes flashed for a split second, and Taylor knew there was no taking it back.

Robert was the kidnapper.

And he knew Taylor knew it.

She went to draw her gun—but he slammed into her, knocking it from her hand. It clattered on the floor, out of reach. Taylor tried to get away, but Robert was too fast. He grabbed hold of her and threw her against the counter. Taylor's head spun as he pinned her down.

She was trapped.

"You're not going anywhere," Robert breathed, his face right in hers.

Taylor squirmed, but she couldn't get away. Robert was much stronger than she was. He grabbed her shirt, and her heart hammered.

"I won't let you go," he hissed, his eyes filled with fire.

In the same fluid movement, he knocked the wind out of her. Taylor hit the ground hard, unable to breathe. She tried to roll over, but Robert stood over her, his eyes dark and expressionless. He grabbed her by the wrist and pulled her to her feet.

Taylor tried to fight him off, but he was too strong. He propelled her toward the back room door, and she pushed against him, but he was impenetrable.

Taylor felt the back door behind her. She knew that was her only way out.

She swung around, grabbed the doorknob, and twisted.

She let out a cry as the door flew open. She turned to Robert, her eyes wide.

A stench clogged her throat as she saw what was behind the door. Horror filled her—but then, a sharp pain struck the back of her head, and everything went black.

CHAPTER TWENTY FIVE

Wesley's phone beeped in his ear as he stood outside of the police station, the blazing sun hot on his black sweatshirt. He had no idea where Taylor had gone, and no matter how many times he tried to call her, her phone would just endlessly ring until it hit the voicemail.

"This is Taylor Sage. Leave a message and I'll get back to you. Thanks."

Wesley hung up without leaving a message. It wasn't like Taylor to not answer her phone within three rings, and letting it go to voicemail was beyond out of character.

Something was wrong.

He'd spent the morning mostly making phone calls and house visits, learning nothing new about the missing girls. Then, Taylor had disappeared. He'd asked around the station, but no one had seen her in a while. Maybe she was just off talking to someone, but considering she wasn't answering, he was sure something wasn't right.

He tried Taylor's number again, but still, nothing. He paced up and down the station's front entrance, his mind racing, before he went back into the cramped and muggy police station.

Taylor was a good agent. If he knew her at all, then he knew she'd probably found something out—and decided to run it down on her own. But if she wasn't answering, then maybe she was in danger.

Wesley had to get into her mind, discover what she'd discovered. And the only way he could think to do that was to re-examine the clues they had on the case.

He brought out a file with all the information on the missing girls. There had to be something he wasn't seeing here, something Taylor had noticed that he hadn't. He took out their photos and flipped through them. All dark-haired, fair-skinned, and light-eyed young women. With the slight gap in their teeth, as Taylor had pointed out. He stopped on the photo of the most recent missing girl: Katelyn. She smiled bright, and there was a slight gap between her two front teeth.

The gears in Wesley's head began to turn. Before they'd been interrupted earlier, Taylor had suggested looking into deaths on the island in the past year. The profile she'd been building on the kidnapper suggested he may have been trying to replace a woman he knew in real life with these girls, who had similar features. If the gap tooth was one of them, that could narrow down Wesley's search.

Opening up his phone, he opened up a site with all of Brock Island's obituaries. He scrolled through the names, but couldn't find anything. He was just looking at photos of people who'd died and it all made his heart hurt. As a father, death wasn't something he liked thinking about, but as an agent, it dominated most of his life.

He closed his eyes and tried to think of what else they could do. Then he looked up recent obituaries.

One of them was Patricia Marie Gable, who'd left behind a husband.

She had light eyes and a gap tooth.

Damn. Wesley's mind raced. This could be their guy. Knowing Taylor, she would have already seen this and was probably there by herself.

Wesley hurried over to Sheriff Garth's office and knocked on the door, opening it. Garth was behind his desk, and he looked up with a sour expression on his face.

"Garth," Wesley said, "do you know where Robert Gable lives?"

Garth nodded. "Yeah, why?" he said.

"I have reason to believe that he's the kidnapper," Wesley said.

Garth's face darkened. "What makes you think that?"

"That's not important," Wesley said. "I need to know where he is."

"He owns the bait and tackle shop down by the southern pier," Garth said. "You'll have to follow the road south out of town. It's about ten minutes in. You can't miss it."

Wesley thanked him and hurried out, jogging across the road to the police car they'd loaned him. If he was right, then Robert Gable was the kidnapper. Any evidence he could gain on the investigation would be invaluable.

The drive down to Gable's shop was quick, and Wesley slowed down as he approached the shop. He knew he had to handle this with care. He couldn't just walk up to the man's shop, guns blazing. Not if Taylor's life was potentially on the line.

The shop was a small one-story building with a tattered sign that read 'Gable's Bait and Tackle' and a large, tarp-covered boat sitting on the pier. Two cars were parked in the front lot, and Wesley desperately hoped that one of them was Robert's.

He parked and shut off the car before checking his gun in the holster at his hip, and then his knife. He took a breath and then stepped out of the car into the blazing sun. He could feel sweat forming on his forehead.

Wesley approached the shop slowly, his eyes scanning everywhere. He hadn't seen anyone, but that didn't mean that they weren't there. And if they were there, it meant that he couldn't take Gable by surprise. A bead of sweat rolled down Wesley's cheek. He couldn't see anyone through the windows.

Now or never.

He pushed open the door and stepped inside.

The small shop was an explosion of fishing rods, life vests, and lures. The small bell above the door jingled as Wesley stepped inside, and a bell on the back wall in the corner jingled, too. Wesley stood there, his eyes scanning for any sign of life—just as a grizzled man in overalls with rain boots stepped in front of him, as if out of nowhere.

"Can I help you?"

Wesley paused. He needed to handle this delicately. The last thing he wanted was to trigger the man and end up having to shoot him. He also needed to know where Taylor was. Everything inside was telling him that she was in here somewhere.

First, he decided to play it casual.

"Morning," he said. "I'm Special Agent Wesley with the FBI. I'm looking into the disappearances of several young women here on the island. Are you Robert Gable?"

The man's face darkened. "Yeah, I'm him. But I don't know anything about that," he said. "I'm just running the family business, here. And I don't know what my family has to do with any of that."

Wesley leveled his gaze at the man, trying to keep his composure.

"You have a family, Mr. Gable?" Wesley asked. "The sheriff mentioned you don't have any children, and your wife passed away."

"She did," Gable said, nodding. "No children. But my wife and I ran the shop. Now, I don't mean to be rude, but can I help you with anything?"

"Actually," Wesley said, "I'd like to look around your shop."

Gable visibly tensed up. "I don't have to let you do that," he said.

"I just want to look around for about five minutes." Wesley wrung his hand along his belt, exposing the gun beneath his sweatshirt for a brief moment.

Gable eyed him warily. "Yeah, okay, sure," Gable said. "I guess you can look. It's not like I've got anything to hide."

He waved his hand at the aisles. Wesley walked past him, scanning everywhere. Gable was probably trying to keep a casual attitude, but Wesley could tell he was nervous. Wesley moved around the shop, taking in the various items for sale. The air was thick with the stench of fish and worms and bait.

Behind the back counter was a closed door. Wesley walked over to it and tried the handle. It was locked.

"What's in there?" he asked Gable.

"Just storage," Gable said. "I keep all my supplies in there."

Wesley nodded. "Mind if I take a look?"

"Sure," Gable said, shrugging.

It was casual. Too casual. But Wesley went to open the door—just he was lunged at from behind.

Wesley had felt it coming—and dodged out of the way of Gable's attack, letting him fall face-first into the door. Gable stumbled back and turned. Wesley tried to get his gun out, but the old man tackled him with a shocking amount of strength. Wesley's back slammed against the cash counter, and he found his arms pinned above his head by Gable.

But Wesley was trained. His knee went right up, into Gable's gut. Gable's eyes went wide and he exhaled, letting go of Wesley and going to his knees. Wesley jumped back and leveled his gun at Gable.

"Where are they?" he asked. "Where are the girls, Gable? Where is Taylor?"

"Forget it!" Gable shouted. "They're mine, and you're not taking them!"

Wesley's hand tightened on the grip of his gun. He wanted to shoot him. He wanted to put a bullet right between Gable's eyes. But he couldn't. He had to be careful.

"Do not mess with me," Wesley said. "It's over, Gable. You've been caught. Give it up."

Gable held his head low. He wasn't talking. Wesley, still with his gun on him, went behind his back and pulled out his cuffs. He slapped them on Gable's wrist, then yanked him to his feet.

Wesley didn't need Gable to tell him more. The answers he was seeking were almost certainly behind that door. But when Wesley went to open it, it wouldn't budge.

"The key," Wesley said. "Where is it?"

Gable didn't answer.

A rush of anger struck Wesley's chest. He pulled out his gun and stuck it in Gable's jugular.

"Tell me where the key is."

"It's in the desk," Gable said. "In the drawer."

Wesley moved around the sales counter and found the small, metal desk in the corner. He opened the drawer and, sure enough, there was the key. He hurried back to the door and unlocked it, then turned and leveled his gun on Gable.

"I'm going in now," Wesley said. "And if you try anything, I will not hesitate to shoot you."

Gable nodded, lowering his head and shutting his eyes. Wesley didn't know if he was crying or if he was just afraid.

"Good," Wesley said. He pulled Gable through the door and into the dark room.

The room was completely dark. Wesley's eyes couldn't adjust for a few moments, and then he heard a tiny whimper. And the smell—it was awful, like pungent, rotting flesh and death.

Someone had died in here.

Wesley shoved Gable to the floor and turned on the light.

What he saw made his blood run cold.

Katelyn, alive and trembling, was tied to a chair with fishing line pressed so deep into her skin she was turning red. Taylor was unconscious, sprawled out on the floor next to her.

And in the back of the room was a barrel, one Wesley suspected was responsible for the smell of dead flesh.

Wesley didn't have time to think—he hurried over to Taylor and moved her on her back.

She was still breathing.

Thank God.

He looked up at Katelyn. "Are you okay, sweetheart?"

"P-please," she whimpered, "get me out of here!"

Wesley drew his knife and began snipping Katelyn's restraints, freeing her. Once she was able to move, he went back to Taylor and shook her. She didn't wake, and panic flooded him. He looked around the room. How had he been able to keep them in here so publicly? But then he noticed the soundproofing pads on the walls. Gable must've spent weeks soundproofing this place, turning it into his torture box.

He shook Taylor again until slowly, her eyes opened. They fell right on him.

"Wesley?" she asked.

"It's over, Sage," he said. "It's over."

CHAPTER TWENTY SIX

Robert Gable sat across from Taylor in the interrogation room back at the police station, and her blood was running hot in her veins. He'd bested her before, but she felt a strong sense of justice surge through her now that he was here, right where he belonged. Taylor had a bandage wrapped around her head from where Robert had hit her, and it hurt like hell—but he was caught.

Still, it didn't just erase everything that had happened. Nothing would. They'd been able to save Katelyn. But Amy—her body had been found in a barrel in the back, chopped up into pieces and stuffed in a garbage bag.

Taylor would never forget the smell.

"The other girls," Taylor said. It was hard to look this man in the eyes. "Where are they?"

Robert had grown cavalier since his arrest. A half smile tugged at his lips, and he shook his head. "Dead. All of them."

Taylor's stomach curled. She wanted to reach across the table and make him pay. But she kept herself together. He wasn't even trying to hide what he'd done, and somehow, that made this all the more chilling.

"Where?" she asked.

"They're in barrels off the coast of the island. Sea probably washed them away by now. But who knows, really?"

Taylor's hands vibrated. To confirm, she needed to know which of the missing girls he really did kill. She brought out the photos of Jessica Clements, Brenda Grimmie, and Samantha Skelly. She slid the photos across the table, and Robert's beady eyes fell on them.

"Did you kill all these girls?" Taylor asked.

He looked up at her, emotionless. "I did." He didn't blink. Taylor's heart nearly stopped beating. He didn't show remorse. He didn't show any emotion.

He was a monster.

"And how did you kill them?" Taylor asked. She needed to know.

"I used a fishing line to strangle them, then cut their bodies with a saw so they'd fit into the barrels. They were petite girls, but not that petite. I had to work around fitting them in."

It all made Taylor sick. "Why? Why did you do this? Because they looked like your wife?"

That seemed to make him clam up. Robert's eyes flared against Taylor's, finally showing a hint of emotion—but it was all anger, all disgust. No empathy for the lives he'd senselessly stolen.

"None of them were Patricia," he said. "None of them."

Taylor leaned forward. "You wanted to replace her, didn't you?"

"They weren't her!" he screamed.

Taylor didn't flinch. He could yell, raise his voice all he wanted. But he was finished.

"I know," Taylor said. "And you could never replace her. So you killed them. You killed them all."

"One day, I was going to let one of them live," he said. "One of them..." He began to crumble, eyes pinched shut, face twisted in anger. "Patricia—she cheated so many times. She used me. Left me to dry. And she would hit me so much. I needed her to love me. I..."

Taylor was sick from it all. So, that was the story. Robert had never recovered from his wife's infidelity and abuse, and so when she died, he was left with no closure. It manifested in a sick and twisted way; it seemed he had been chasing the image of his wife when she was young, when they were both young.

She understood why Robert was the way he was now. He would rot in jail forever, where he belonged, and she was thankful for that.

But there was one question that still weighed heavy on Taylor's mind.

She glanced over her shoulder, at the door to the interrogation room. No one would come in; she'd asked Wesley to let her talk to Robert alone, and he promised to give her some time. So, she took out her phone, and opened up a photo of Angie.

She showed it to Robert, her heart in her throat, praying he might know something. Even if the answer was that Angie was in a barrel somewhere—at least then, Taylor would know the truth. She could bring answers home to her parents.

But no recognition crossed Robert's face. "She isn't one of mine," he said.

Taylor's world came crashing down. She felt like she might pass out. It was just as she'd feared.

Of course Robert had nothing to do with Angie.

He was old enough, yes, but he'd only been active since his wife died. It had been twenty years since Angie vanished. These two cases; they weren't connected at all.

So why? Taylor asked herself. Why did the cards lead her here? What about the symbol by the rocks that she'd seen in her memory with Angie? Was it all a delusion? Taylor didn't know. She didn't know anything. She never even found the symbol here, so maybe her mind did fabricate the whole thing.

Either way, there were no answers left for her here.

She stood up and left the interrogation room, having Robert Gable's confession on record. The Amy Schuler case was closed.

But Taylor was leaving Brock Island emptier than she'd ever been in her life.

EPILOGUE

Taylor's dad kicked his feet up on the ottoman in the living room, opening a book on his lap as the fireplace reflected on his glasses. On the couch, Taylor was curled up in the corner while her mom sat on the other side, sketching in her art book.

The TV was on, playing the news, but nobody was watching.

Least of all Taylor.

She was grateful to be home with her parents, and even more grateful that her father was recovering soundly. Still, Taylor blamed herself for everything, and she couldn't help but feel heavy with guilt considering she had come home empty-handed. There was no information on Angie, but they hadn't talked about it yet. When Taylor returned home, her mom knew right away; she could tell by the look on Taylor's face that she'd found nothing. And her father had said he wasn't mad at her and didn't blame her for the heart attack, but Taylor couldn't accept that.

Taylor leaned forward and grabbed the remote off the table, turning off the TV. Her parents both looked up from their books.

"What is it, sweetie?" her dad asked.

Taylor turned to face them. This was the moment she'd been dreading; she needed to talk about Angie. Taylor knew she wouldn't be able to live with herself if she didn't.

"I'm just... sorry," Taylor confessed. "I'm sorry, Dad, for stressing you out."

He sighed and took off his glasses. "Taylor, I already told you. It wasn't your fault. Your mother was right—I'd been eating too much salty food. It was only a matter of time before my heart gave me a reminder, you know?"

"But I put a lot of pressure on you," Taylor insisted. "And now... we don't have any answers. You were right…"

"I think you did a good job," her mother said. "I know it's hard for you to accept, honey, but everything happens for a reason. I think, maybe, you're outgrowing this case. It was time."

Taylor blinked back tears. "I know, but..." She shook her head, and bit her lip. "What if she's still out there somewhere? What if she's still alive?"

Taylor's parents both got up and sat down on either side of her. Her father put a hand on her shoulder.

"Taylor, honey," he said. "If she was alive out there, she would've found her way home. Wherever she is, she would've found her way home. Angie loved all of us. Especially you."

Taylor couldn't believe it. This was the first time in years her father had been so open to talking about Angie. "Dad, you never talk about her like this," Taylor said.

He laughed, accentuating the crow's feet at the corners of his eyes. "Well, I've been thinking," he said. "I'm a psychologist, but I've been doing the opposite of what I tell my patients for years. I've been suppressing Angie's memory, sometimes so much that I don't even want to say her name. As unhealthy as it is to think about it too much and obsess, it's also unhealthy to pretend it never happened. Besides..." He trailed off. "I have to hold onto the good memories I have of her."

Taylor's mom smiled too, and reached over to grab his hand. "That's right, Randall," she said. "Let's not be sad tonight. Let's stay positive. Let's celebrate."

Taylor smiled through her tears. "Celebrate?"

"Yes," her mother said. "We're celebrating what would've been Angie's thirty-seventh birthday."

Taylor checked the date on her phone. Wow. She hadn't even realized. It was October 1st, Angie's birthday.

"I love you, and I'll never forget you," her mom whispered, bringing her necklace to her mouth and kissing it.

"Happy Birthday, Angel," her dad mumbled. "We love you."

Taylor hugged them both. Taylor's mom kissed her forehead and gave her a squeeze. "I'm going to go to bed," she said. "You two stay up as late as you'd like, okay?"

"'Night, Mom," Taylor said.

The next hour or so, she and her dad sat and reminisced. Taylor could hardly believe the change in her dad; he was much more open and genuine than ever before. It made her realize that both her parents had been going through a far worse time than she had over the years. Taylor could only imagine how much pain they'd been in, and she hoped that someday she'd be able to bring them the closure they deserved, even if it did only prove that Angie had been murdered.

Taylor only knew one thing for certain; she wasn't going to give up. Angie was her sister, and she was going to find her.

"I really wish she was here," Taylor said.

"Me too," her father said, sitting up straight. "But I'm thankful that I still have you."

Taylor smiled. "Thanks, Dad."

He got up and walked over to the fireplace, leaving Taylor alone on the couch with her thoughts. She was glad that this long-standing issue between her and her dad was resolved, but it didn't make her feel any better about Angie.

Her dad left the room, and Taylor went over to the bookshelf by the fireplace. In it were old photo albums. Taylor knew it was past time she looked through them.

She grabbed one and brought it to the couch. Opening it up on her lap, she began to flip through the pages. There were pictures of her back when she was a toddler, of her with her sister, and even a few of her with her father. She didn't remember any of these photos being taken.

She paused at another photo.

It was a picture of her and Angie, taken when Taylor was ten and Angie was twelve. Angie was smiling brightly, but Taylor was playing with the bottom of her hair and looking away from the camera.

Taylor remembered that day in the park. They had been playing with their new scooters. Taylor had gotten really good at it on the first try, but Angie ended up breaking her big toe. Angie had been in the hospital for a bit, but Taylor didn't remember ever being there with her.

Taylor flipped to another page, where there was a picture of her and her sister on the shore of a lake, standing side by side. Angie looked exactly like Taylor, but her smile was a little bigger. She was squinting at the sun and watching seagulls fly overhead. This beach wasn't like the one on Brock Island. No, this was a different place they had vacationed one time, and Taylor hadn't thought about it in years.

She flipped to another photo, and it showed Taylor and Angie in front of a log cabin. Right—Taylor remembered one summer, they hadn't been able to get the Brock Island beach house, and so Taylor's dad had searched for another spot for them to vacation. It ended up being a log cabin in the woods, right by the shore of a lake.

Taylor remembered being creeped out by it. The cabin's weathered wooden walls had creaked in the wind, and their reflection in the windows looked distorted, like demons. Plus, it had been so cold—their family had to huddle by the fireplace every night to keep warm.

Taylor couldn't believe how different all of these photos were. It was like looking at two different worlds, because the Taylor in all of these photos was so different. She was drawn back to that log cabin, to that creepy place. Taylor flipped to another photo.

It was her and Angie on the shore of the lake again.

And in the background were rocks off the shore. One of them had white writing on it.

Taylor's heart stopped.

She leaned in closer to see if she was imagining things.

But no. Whatever the rock said wasn't clear, but it looked strikingly similar to the memory Taylor thought she'd had about Brock Island.

It hit her hard, like a punch to the gut. She hadn't gotten the image in her heard wrong—she had gotten the *location* wrong.

It was real.

This place was real.

And Taylor had to find it.

***

Taylor's heart pounded. The woods were terrifying in the dead of night. A maze of branches and twigs, dead leaves and wilted flowers, and unidentifiable objects crowding the forest floor. The night smelled of damp earth and rot.

But Taylor couldn't wait.

She had to find the log cabin. She had to know if it was real.

She'd been able to get the name of the company who had rented out the cabins from her father; he'd had to dig back in twenty years' worth of emails, but he still had one. He remembered it so well because, according to him, it had been the worst renting experience of his life. Unprofessional staff, plus the cabin had not been as advertised. It was supposed to be a lake house paradise, but instead had been more of a derelict cabin.

He'd been entirely opposed to Taylor going after it at all, let alone by herself at night, but he also knew that at this point, there was no stopping her when she had her mind on something. Taylor had to see it for herself.

And besides, she was armed.

She could handle whatever the woods threw at her.

Her phone in her hand, the light from the screen guided her through the pitch-black forest. With only a few hours left of the night, she had to hurry—it would get light soon. With every step, she wondered if someone was watching her from the shadows. She ran her hand over the cold metal of her gun.

"I can do this," she said to herself, though her voice came out weak and shaky. She cleared her throat and spoke again. "I can do this." This time her voice was stronger, more determined.

Taylor walked around a tree trunk, then stopped. She heard a rustling noise behind her. She held her breath and turned around. But there was nothing there, just the thick rows of trees, swaying in the wind. Just a forest. Nothing to worry about. She turned back around and continued walking, her heart pounding in her chest.

Soon, the sound of waves gently lapping the shore filled her ears.

The lake.

According to her GPS, the cabin should have been close. There were several in the area, but Taylor had one in mind.

She came across a sign. PRIVATE PROPERTY. NO TRESSPASSING.

She was getting close.

She walked on.

And then she saw it.

It was just as she remembered it.

The weathered, brown logs looked like the arms of a monster, reaching out to engulf her. She could see the window of her old room, its glass broken. The door hung off of its hinges, and the roof was falling apart. It was real.

Taylor didn't know how to feel anymore. It felt as though her whole world was turning upside down. After leaving Brock Island, she'd been convinced that all of this tarot stuff had led her nowhere but on a path to insanity. But this reaffirmed her that there was hope. It wasn't dead, not yet.

Her legs were shaking. She walked to the door. The familiar feeling of leaves crunching under her feet filled the silence.

She reached for the doorknob, but froze.

On the shingle of a broken window was a symbol, scribbled in chalk.

The circle.

The squiggled line beneath.

Taylor sucked in a breath. She hesitated. She didn't know what she'd find behind that door, but one thing was certain.

It could change her life forever.

To be safe, she took out her phone and sent Wesley a quick text, along with her location.

I'm at this cabin in the woods. I think my sister might be here. Back me up if you can.

And that was it.

Taylor faced the door.

A deep breath, and she walked in.

NOW AVAILABLE!

<u>DON'T REMEMBER</u>
(A Taylor Sage FBI Suspense Thriller—Book 5)

The survivor of a new serial killer remembers but one harrowing detail: his eerie voice. With only this strange clue—and an equally perplexing lead from the tarot reader—FBI agent Taylor Sage must race to stop this murderer before he leaves another body in his wake.

"Molly Black has written a taut thriller that will keep you on the edge of your seat… I absolutely loved this book and can't wait to read the next book in the series!"
—Reader review for Girl One: Murder

DON'T REMEMBER is book #5 of a brand-new series by critically acclaimed and #1 bestselling mystery and suspense author Molly Black.

When her most promising lead turns out to be a dead end, Taylor knows she must think outside of the box, must think how he thinks. But the killer always seems to be two steps ahead, and time is running out—fast.

Will Taylor manage to stop him before the next victim is killed?

A page-turning and harrowing crime thriller featuring a brilliant and tortured FBI agent, the TAYLOR SAGE series is a riveting mystery, packed with non-stop action, suspense, twists and turns, revelations, and driven by a breakneck pace that will keep you flipping pages late into the night. Fans of Rachel Caine, Teresa Driscoll and Robert Dugoni are sure to fall in love.

Book #6 in the series—DON'T TELL—is now also available!

“I binge read this book. It hooked me in and didn't stop till the last few pages… I look forward to reading more!”
—Reader review for Found You

“I loved this book! Fast-paced plot, great characters and interesting insights into investigating cold cases. I can't wait to read the next book!”
—Reader review for Girl One: Murder

“Very good book… You will feel like you are right there looking for the kidnapper! I know I will be reading more in this series!”
—Reader review for Girl One: Murder

“This is a very well written book and holds your interest from page 1… Definitely looking forward to reading the next one in the series, and hopefully others as well!”
—Reader review for Girl One: Murder

“Wow, I cannot wait for the next in this series. Starts with a bang and just keeps going.”
—Reader review for Girl One: Murder

“Well written book with a great plot, one that will keep you up at night. A page turner!”
—Reader review for Girl One: Murder

“A great suspense that keeps you reading… can't wait for the next in this series!”
—Reader review for Found You

“Sooo soo good! There are a few unforeseen twists… I binge read this like I binge watch Netflix. It just sucks you in.”
—Reader review for Found You

Molly Black

Bestselling author Molly Black is author of the MAYA GRAY FBI suspense thriller series, comprising nine books (and counting); of the RYLIE WOLF FBI suspense thriller series, comprising six books (and counting); of the TAYLOR SAGE FBI suspense thriller series, comprising six books (and counting); and of the KATIE WINTER FBI suspense thriller series, comprising nine books (and counting).

An avid reader and lifelong fan of the mystery and thriller genres, Molly loves to hear from you, so please feel free to visit www.mollyblackauthor.com to learn more and stay in touch.

BOOKS BY MOLLY BLACK

MAYA GRAY MYSTERY SERIES
GIRL ONE: MURDER (Book #1)
GIRL TWO: TAKEN (Book #2)
GIRL THREE: TRAPPED (Book #3)
GIRL FOUR: LURED (Book #4)
GIRL FIVE: BOUND (Book #5)
GIRL SIX: FORSAKEN (Book #6)
GIRL SEVEN: CRAVED (Book #7)
GIRL EIGHT: HUNTED (Book #8)
GIRL NINE: GONE (Book #9)

RYLIE WOLF FBI SUSPENSE THRILLER
FOUND YOU (Book #1)
CAUGHT YOU (Book #2)
SEE YOU (Book #3)
WANT YOU (Book #4)
TAKE YOU (Book #5)
DARE YOU (Book #6)

TAYLOR SAGE FBI SUSPENSE THRILLER
DON'T LOOK (Book #1)
DON'T BREATHE (Book #2)
DON'T RUN (Book #3)
DON'T FLINCH (Book #4)
DON'T REMEMBER (Book #5)
DON'T TELL (Book #6)

KATIE WINTER FBI SUSPENSE THRILLER
SAVE ME (Book #1)
REACH ME (Book #2)
HIDE ME (Book #3)
BELIEVE ME (Book #4)
HELP ME (Book #5)
FORGET ME (Book #6)
HOLD ME (Book #7)

PROTECT ME (Book #8)
REMEMBER ME (Book #9)

www.ingramcontent.com/pod-product-compliance
Lightning Source LLC
Chambersburg PA
CBHW020322030826
48979CB00022B/704